The
Last Hope
in
Hopetown

The
Last Hope
in
Hopetown

MARIA TUREAUD

LITTLE, BROWN AND COMPANY

New York   Boston

Little, Brown and Company
Hachette Book Group
1290 Avenue of the Americas, New York, NY 10104
Visit us at LBYR.com

First Edition: October 2022

Little, Brown and Company is a division of Hachette Book Group, Inc. The Little, Brown name and logo are trademarks of Hachette Book Group, Inc.

The publisher is not responsible for websites (or their content) that are not owned by the publisher.

Library of Congress Cataloging-in-Publication Data
Names: Tureaud, Maria, author.
Title: The last hope in Hopetown / Maria Tureaud.
Description: First edition. | New York ; Boston : Little, Brown and Company, 2022. | Audience: Ages 8–12. | Summary: Twelve-year-old Sophie and her 300-year-old best vampire friend Delphine break into a secret government facility to find a cure for the illness causing vampires to go rogue.
Identifiers: LCCN 2021053744 | ISBN 9780316368452 (hardcover) | ISBN 9780316368667 (ebook)
Subjects: CYAC: Vampires—Fiction. | Adoption—Fiction. | Mothers—Fiction. | LCGFT: Novels.
Classification: LCC PZ7.1.T873 Las 2022 | DDC [Fic]—dc23
LC record available at https://lccn.loc.gov/2021053744

ISBNs: 978-0-316-36845-2 (hardcover),
978-0-316-36866-7 (ebook)

Printed in the United States of America

LSC-C

Printing 1, 2022

For my sister, Sara. It was
always just us—you, me, and our
imaginations.

Chapter 1

I have two moms.

They adopted me like five years ago, when I was seven. But that wasn't why Laura from Child Protective Services sat in my living room when I should've been headed to Chuck's Chocolate House with my best friend, Delphine. No.

She was there because my parents are vampires.

"How about school, Sophie?" Laura asked, little finger pointing to the ceiling as she delicately sipped tea from Mama's treasured porcelain tea set.

I liked her. She'd been my case worker for three years and treated my parents like humans. She even drank tea correctly, which made Mama very happy. Though I'm pretty sure Laura learned how just so Mama would like her.

"School's good," I replied brightly—maybe a little too brightly. The sooner Laura decided everything was fine, the sooner I'd be free. It was Saturday, for crying out loud. "Solid Bs."

"Ready for seventh grade?" Laura asked, smiling as I tapped my foot. I did that a lot. Mama said I was always fidgeting, ready to "flee the palace," but my other mom, the Duke, called it "battle ready."

"Yep." I nodded. Delphine was probably wondering where I was, but she didn't own a cell phone. This was exactly why she needed one—because CPS didn't exactly let anyone know when they were showing up.

"All right." Chuckling, Laura put down the teacup and grabbed her iPad. "Mom got a new doll, huh?"

My nose wrinkled as I turned to peek at the creepy thing propped up on the end table. Mama loved antique dolls, especially French ones. Preferably dressed in her favorite color—pink. Like the living room walls. And the fancy, old-timey, French-style furniture.

"Yeah. She said it reminded her of someone she used to know." I couldn't remember who, but I was sure Mama had said. She liked to name-drop, even though I always had to open a search browser on the internet to figure out who the heck her friends were. I even found Mama on there—well, sort of. She'd had lots of names, because vampires used to change them every ten to fifteen years and move away so humans wouldn't wonder why they weren't getting old. One of those names was Marie Thérèse Louise de Savoie-Carignan, the Princesse de Lamballe, a friend of Queen Marie Antoinette. It was a mouthful. That's why my moms chose Dawes as our family name. It was the name Mama was born with, and she wanted me to be part of her family heritage.

"I'm sure. That's the amazing thing about vampires, isn't it? All that history," Laura said, swiping her fingers over the screen of the iPad. "All right, Sophie. Real quick and I'll be out of your hair."

I sat up straight and forced my foot to stop tapping. Five minutes. That's all the questionnaire ever took. Then I could meet Delphine and tell her all about the letter in my back pocket.

"Has everything been normal at home?" Laura asked.

"Yes." Twenty seconds gone. Four minutes forty seconds to go.

"Any change in circumstance?"

That meant jobs and things. "Nope. All good."

"Have your parents been keeping the curfew?"

"Yes." Though the Duke did take me for late-night ice cream twice a week, she never stepped foot out of the car. No one ever saw. It was our secret.

"Any changes in behavior?"

Mama chose that moment to sashay into the living room, with a bright: "*Voilà!* I made cookies."

Inside, I groaned. That five minutes could turn into twenty if Mama got talking.

"Mmm." Laura made that whole *ew, gross, but I don't want to be rude* face.

Mama's cookies were The Worst. She loved to bake, but since she didn't eat human food, she didn't know everything she cooked tasted like chalk. Mainly because I never told her.

4

"Thanks, Mama," I said, reaching out to grab one of the lumpy, burnt cookies as she offered the tray. I'd tried to show her how to bake them right, but her eyes got all bloody—vampires cried blood—and then I felt bad because she got upset if I didn't like something, and I just wanted her to always be happy.

She was the best. Always trying so hard to fit in with our human neighbors, even though I loved Mama just the way she was. Because she was my mom.

"Oh, I couldn't possibly—" Laura tried to tactfully decline, but Mama cut her off with an insistent chuckle.

"Come, come, Ms. Snyder. They're gluten-free, nut free, and chocolate chip." Mama grinned, and her pink lipstick shone bright against super pale skin. She wore a ruffle-necked blouse and a swirly pink skirt that sat really high on her waist. It came to mid-calf, but poofed out thanks to a fluffy underskirt. She looked like one of those housewives from the old movies she loved to watch—the black-and-white ones from the fifties. She even wore a set of pearls.

Laura smiled a little and politely took a cookie. She knew the drill.

Mama stood, smiling. Waiting. Her smile dimming with each passing second as Laura sat there. Not eating.

"They're really good, Mama," I said, trying to distract everyone.

But Mama still stood there. Watching Laura. Until Laura finally took a tentative bite.

"Mmm," Laura murmured around the crumbly, burnt cookie. "Very good."

Liar. But that was all right, because Mama's smile grew really wide.

"Wonderful! I'll be back with some lemonade."

"Oh, we're almost done here," Laura said, her eyes going a bit panicky as the blood drained from her face.

"Then you'll take some lemonade to go!" With a happy twirl, Mama sashayed for the door, humming an out-of-key tune all the way to the kitchen.

"Okay." With a sigh, Laura turned her attention back to the iPad as I shoved the rest of the cookie into my pocket. I'd trash it later. It really was pretty bad. "No change in behavior then. Let me just tick that off. How about mood swings?"

"Nothing out of the ordinary," I replied. Mama was Mama, filled with so much love and empathy and worry. But the Duke was solid as a rock. They were a really great team.

"Good, good. All right, Sophie. I think I have everything I need."

I wanted to ask how much longer this would go on for. Not just this visit, but in general. These checkups really only started when the first vampires began going rogue like three years ago. Which seemed silly at the time, because most of those cases were on the West Coast. But that was then. Now there were news stories almost every day about rogue vampires in the Northeast.

My moms told me having a CPS agent was for my safety, to make sure everything was all right and that they weren't affected by whatever was making others turn on their human families and friends. But I knew it upset them. Dinners were always weird after Laura stopped by—the Duke got quieter, and Mama filled the silence with chatter.

That's why I always insisted on playing a family board game and letting them read me a bedtime story on those nights. Because being together as a family always made them happier...even if I was way too old to be tucked in.

"Can I go?" I asked, already half off my chair.

"Sure thing. What adventures am I keeping you from today?" Packing her things into a sleek black messenger bag, Laura stood, glancing from the cookie in her hand to the ornate glass coffee table and back to the cookie again.

"Just hanging out with a friend. Here," I said, taking the cookie from her hand. I shoved it in my growing, gross cookie-stash pocket, and she relaxed with a smile.

"Thank you."

"You got it."

Mama called something from the kitchen, and Laura tensed again.

"Don't worry," I said, winking. "The lemonade is fine. The Duke bought it."

"Oh." Laura blushed a little and rose from her chair, slinging her bag over her shoulder. "Then lead the way."

Leading the way meant sticking around for longer, and that made my foot tap. But I stood and walked into the kitchen ahead of Laura. I guess I could wait five more minutes, but I'd really have to excuse myself as soon as possible.

Me and Delphine had very important things to do today.

Like stop at the blood bank to pick up my moms' weekly order.

And decide what to do about the letter in my back pocket. The one from my birth mom.

Chapter 2

The sun was hotter than a jalapeño on pizza. It was only spring, but it felt like summer. Vamps weren't fans of the heat, so Mama kept the air-conditioning at a cool sixty degrees. I didn't even think to change out of my faded black band sweater and ripped jeans, but halfway down the block the heat hit me like a ton of bricks.

The day before had been maybe fifty degrees and gray as a thunderstorm, but today my neighbors were out in force, mowing lawns and weeding their flower beds as if the landscape police would pop out of nowhere and call them lazy. Lawn after lawn, cute colonial redbrick house after redbrick house, white picket fence after white picket fence, with bright rainbow flags proudly displayed. We lived in an LGBTQ+ neighborhood, but we were the only vampire family on the street.

Hopetown was old but still looked good. Its brick homes and businesses were super pretty, and the town was known as an American Revolution time capsule kind of place. Which was probably why so many vampires decided to call it home—it reminded them of old times.

Rolling my sleeves, I hurried down Freedom Row and took a right onto Liberty Avenue. The Duke always said she chose our home just for the address: 617 Freedom Row, Hopetown, Pennsylvania. Freedom and hope. A nice sigh of relief as vampires left the darkness almost twenty years ago to walk in the light with humans. No more shadows. No more living in secret, in myth and lore and legend. They were real, they were here, and they wanted to pay taxes like everyone else. Which I never got. Why would anyone want to give their money away?

It wasn't long before I left my neighborhood

behind and crossed Main Street to the cobbled plaza in the center of town, a perfect pedestrian area lined with benches and trees and flower baskets.

In the plaza, I spotted Delphine standing in front of Chuck's Chocolate House, looking completely out of place in a blue ankle-length skirt and crisp white blouse. She could've stepped right out of a painting, or one of the local history tours.

Or maybe I was the one out of place, with my simple black bob haircut, frumpy band sweater, and ripped jeans. I definitely wasn't cool and mysterious like Delphine.

Then again, she was a three-hundred-year-old vampire stuck in a twelve-year-old's body. She even held a fancy-looking white umbrella to shade her auburn ringlets, but not because she needed to. Vampires didn't actually hate the sun, or *need* to stay away from it. Being a vampire wasn't like the movies. They could walk around in the daytime just like anyone. No. Delphine brought an umbrella with her everywhere because that was the fashion three hundred years ago.

"As I live and breathe," Delphine drawled, her

dark brown eyes lighting up as I ran across the street. "Sophie Dawes. I thought I'd perish in this here heat waiting for you to grace me with your presence."

She was so dramatic. "Sorry. CPS made a surprise house call."

And just like that, Delphine's pale white face screwed up and she snapped her umbrella shut.

"I could've texted, but you'd have to get a phone first," I continued.

"Fuss and nonsense," Delphine said. "I can't abide all this technology. Why on God's green Earth did CPS make a house call?"

"Who knows?"

"Busybody government types poking their noses where they don't belong. I suppose my parents will be getting a visit from APS shortly." With a sigh, Delphine pursed her bloodred lips. Her Adult Protective Services agent was about as rude as Laura was nice. "You'd think I spent my days just waiting for my parents to fall asleep so I could stick a straw in their veins and drain them."

There weren't many kid vampires. They weren't born, like humans, but made. And it was against the Vampire Morality Code—which was kind of like their laws—to turn a kid into a vampire. They never grew up, not just their bodies, but their minds. Delphine would always be twelve. She just sounded older because that's how kids talked back when she was human.

"Come on. I need an iced hot chocolate," I said with a sigh, walking around Delphine so I could grab the door. It was way too warm for anything hot.

"Rough morning, I assume." Delphine followed as I entered the dark, ambient café. Chuck's Chocolate House had the best coffee and cocoa, muffins and cupcakes. Groups of high schoolers sat in clusters, between tables packed with moms playing catch-up with friends and dads treating their kids to a sugar rush. The inside was all dark polished wood with burnt-orange art and tablecloths. Mama always loved to bring me here. She said the old-timey lamps and real potted ferns reminded her of the art deco style of Paris in the 1930s.

"Definitely a rough morning," I said, getting in line behind a family that couldn't decide between cream-filled muffins or cake pops. Not that I could blame them. The entire café smelled of melted sugar and warm chocolate, so everything was tempting.

"Well, tell me everything."

Reaching into my back pocket, I pulled out the folded letter and handed it to Delphine.

"What's this?" she asked, her eyebrows all scrunched as she took it from me.

"A letter. From...from my birth mom." Biting my lower lip, I took a steady breath through my nose. I mean, my moms had talked about this with me. They'd told me she wanted to get into contact, and I'd said it was okay. But my heart still raced as I watched Delphine's eyes widen.

"Are you sure you want to share this with me?" she asked. I nodded.

Delphine opened the letter with care as I focused on the family ahead of us in line. They chose cake pops, and I stepped up to the counter as they left. Tara Washington—my birth mom—wanted to meet. I tried to smile at the cashier, but my heart wasn't in it. "Hi. Can I get an iced hot chocolate to go?"

The cashier nodded and glanced at Delphine. "Anything for you?"

I groaned as Delphine's attention switched from the letter to the cashier.

"Do you have any O-negative?" Delphine smiled as the cashier's eyes widened. Delphine knew as well as I did that Chuck's didn't sell blood.

"Kidding." With a laugh, Delphine shook her head as the cashier's face turned paler than an egg white. "Though y'all could make so much more money if you catered to *all* your patrons."

"I'm so sorry," said the cashier, and Delphine smiled.

"Don't be. It's not *your* fault."

With a nod, the cashier turned to make my chocolate, and I rolled my eyes.

"I don't get why they can't order from the blood bank," I said, glancing at Delphine—who was back to reading the letter.

"They simply don't have the means to store it. It's all right. Besides, I already ate," she murmured. "Did you show this to your moms?"

"No. I mean, not yet. They know about it, though."

"This really is a sweet letter."

My Darling Sophie,

There's so much to say, but I have no idea how to say it. I'm really glad you're in a loving home, and I'm so grateful your mothers allowed me to write. I know this might seem too little too late, but know that I value you above everything, and giving you up was the hardest decision of my life.

You probably have lots of questions, and I'd love to answer them, hopefully in person—if you're willing to meet me (with your moms, of course! I'd love to get to know them too), and if not, that's okay. Maybe I can send a letter every so often, just like this, and we can maybe meet when, or if, you're ever ready.

All my love,
Tara Washington,
Your mother

A gentle smile lifted the corners of Delphine's lips as she carefully refolded the page, but I scowled.

"I would give anything to see my own mother again. You are so *very* lucky, Sophie! Will you do it?"

That was the big question. Mama and the Duke were my family. I loved them and they loved me, but maybe meeting with my birth mom would make it look as if I didn't want to be part of our family anymore, as if being curious about her meant I didn't love my moms. I wasn't even sure if I *was* curious. I hadn't really thought it was a possibility. My heart fluttered in my chest and my palms got all sweaty.

"I don't know, honestly. It's just...it's complicated," I said. "Things have been hard with all these CPS visits, and...well...what if they don't want to deal with the stress of...of *me* anymore?"

I looked down at my sneakers as Delphine placed a gentle hand on my shoulder. "That would *never* happen. Our families love us and would never give us up. You know that, right?"

Nodding, I sighed. "I know."

"Good. Because the only threat to our families is this whole 'going rogue' business."

I glanced at her and watched as she pressed her lips together.

"No vampires have gone rogue in Hopetown."

"Yet," Delphine said with a sigh, nodding as the barista returned with my drink. I took it with a smile, even if my chest felt all tight. *Yet.* "I swear, the government's turning us rogue on purpose. It's like a big experiment. And if I go rogue, the FBVA will take me and my parents, and I'll never see you again."

I shuddered. This wasn't the first time Delphine had brought up the whole "government doing it on purpose" thing. But the Duke said the new FBVA—Federal Bureau of Vampire Affairs—rehabilitation facility outside Hopetown was paid for by the government with taxpayers' money. There's no way they'd make vampires go rogue only to waste tons of money trying to fix it...right?

"Did Anon715 post again?" I asked quietly, stepping away from the counter. Delphine always checked out their posts on this vampire conspiracy theory online group. It started as a secure support group for vampires, but now they mostly talked about the whole rogue thing—and it was really the only reason Delphine used the internet. That was another thing about being a kid vampire. They were kind of "frozen" in the time period when they were turned, which was why Delphine still wore old-fashioned clothes and hated modern technology.

"Yes, they did," Delphine said with a nod. "Last night. And this time they claimed that there's a cure for going rogue and the government is keeping it secret."

My eyes widened. "Then why wouldn't they use it?"

"My best guess is that they don't want to."

It was also her best guess that the FBVA facility wasn't a rehabilitation center promising to teach vampires how to live among humans again. And that they didn't take entire families so the rogue vampires would be surrounded by people who cared about them.

Because nobody ever came back.

Not the rogue vampires.

Not their families.

And nobody knew what happened to them. But Delphine had a theory, and I was pretty sure she might be right.

The rehab facility was a prison.

Chapter 3

W hat we need to do is talk to this Anon715,"
Delphine said. We had crossed from Chuck's
to the tree-lined Main Street, where cherry blossoms
bloomed pretty and pink, and walked toward the
blood bank. We both had orders to pick up, and I
was glad Delphine shared her umbrella thing as I
sipped my iced hot chocolate. The shade was nice.

"Do you think they'd talk to you?" I asked,
glancing at her shaded face. "I mean, you're a kid."

"As if I could ever forget."

I blinked. Of course she couldn't forget. I
couldn't imagine being twelve years old for three

hundred years. "Obviously. But I meant, would they talk to you because you're technically twelve? Also, wouldn't your parents kill you? I'm not allowed to talk to strangers, especially not online."

"Oh, but Anon715 is a kid as well. I'm certain of it." Delphine turned to me, eyes bright as she gushed. "They use all that modern slang and make sentences with those emoticons—"

"Emojis."

"Whatever they call them now. Anyway, if they're right, it could be huge. Maybe they just need a nudge of 'you can do it' to do the right thing. Imagine! If we were the reason Anon715 went public, we'd be lauded as heroines."

I scanned my brain for "lauded." Maybe it was like applauded? Like people would be happy and cheering? That was the trouble with hanging out with a vampire kid—I needed a dictionary.

"It's kind of exciting," Delphine continued, reaching up to pluck a flower from the cherry tree above us. Around us. I always seemed to walk right where they decided to grow low and annoying. Where one was pushed away, another appeared. Kind of like my life. One problem gone, another appearing.

"Look," I said, brushing aside a low-hanging branch as we made our way down Main Street toward Poplar. "The Duke is helping me with a petition to the governor, asking for answers about what the FBVA are doing with all those kidnapped families. The governor's adopted son is a vampire, and he should be happy to help figure out what's going on. Like what if it happened to his son? That's how things get done, D. Petitions. People in power. Not following a bunch of online theories without evidence."

"Don't you lecture me, Sophie Dawes," she drawled, her native New Orleans accent coming in thick and heavy. "I'm three hundred years your senior."

But that didn't mean I had to do what she said. I only did what grown-ups asked: my moms, my teachers, my CPS agent. But only if what they asked felt right and safe. Delphine might be three hundred, but she was still a kid.

"Yeah, I know. But anyone can put anything they want online. They can lie about their names, their ages, and say there's a cure for going rogue. I just don't want you to get your hopes up."

Sighing heavily, Delphine placed an arm around my shoulder. "Is it a strongly worded petition?"

"Yes!" Digging into my pocket, I pulled out my phone and swiped before finding the document.

"You'll have to read it to me. That screen is far too small, and squinting causes wrinkles, Sophie. Ladies should never wrinkle before thirty."

I smiled. This was why I kept Delphine around. Her weird old-timey talk was hilarious. "Welcome to the twenty-first century, Delphine. Where sunscreen and sunglasses exist. The miracle of modern technology. Also . . . you don't age, silly."

"Pish posh. Let's hear this petition of yours."

"Dear Governor," I began, turning my attention to the screen. "We, the people of the State of Pennsylvania, demand—"

"Demand. A very strong word. Go on." Delphine nodded.

"—the records of those incarcerated by order of the Vampire Rehabilitation Act be made public."

"That's a fine start."

"It goes on with a lot of legal stuff, but then names the families who were taken by the FBVA and never seen again."

"And you're certain the governor will see this and simply...comply?"

"If he loves his own vampire kid, and enough people sign it, then maybe." I watched as Delphine pouted a little, then rushed on before she could try to convince me that her idea was better. "With enough signatures, we can go to the press and get the story out there. That lady from LA did that undercover story about the FBVA facility in California, where everyone was behind bars. It's cruel, D. People hate cruelty."

"That may be, but no one is asking what happens to them once they're taken—"

"Then let's get the petition out there and do this the right way." I cut her off.

Did I want to find out what was happening to

those families? Yes. Did I want to end up like those people? Heck no. And so as long as we lived a quiet life, our family would be safe.

Or, I thought so. I brushed a hand against my back pocket, where my birth mom's letter was safely folded. Delphine was right. I didn't have to deal with that right now.

But the petition, that was something I wanted to do. Something that mattered to me, to my family, and to all vampires.

Delphine went quiet as we reached the busy crosswalk, where the regular, two-laned Main Street spilled onto the wider, four-laned Poplar Street. A modern shopping plaza stood across the busy street with big-name furniture stores, department stores, and a grocery store. There were small shops too, but between a brunch restaurant and a craft store was the blood bank. Its red-and-green SynCorps logo looked super corporate and out of place in the plaza.

"When I was a child," Delphine started talking again as we waited for the signal to change so we could cross the street. Delphine almost never talked about her human life. It was so rare that as she spoke—and

26

that signal refused to flash WALK—I held my breath. "I mean, a real child, before I became a vampire. My birth parents were hauled from my home in New Orleans for crimes they didn't commit by a vampire who called himself Asger. He claimed my mother's family had connections to some old associate of the Van Helsing vampire-hunting network way back when, and so they had to pay the price."

She paused. A chill crept through my sweater, despite the heat. I'd never heard this story before, and I hung on every word. I wanted to tell her to go on—because growing up hearing all the gory details of the French Revolution from Mama made me weird like that—but didn't want to push. Turned out she just needed a second.

"He killed them, plain and simple. And I suppose, in a way, he killed me. Killed what I was, what I might have become." Delphine looked ahead, staring at the crosswalk sign as I now stared at her. "He told me it was a gift, to be a vampire. To live forever and never age. Said making me one of them was the best revenge for my birth parents' so-called crimes. But, Sophie?"

27

That's when she turned, her eyes dark and angry as she locked onto my gaze.

"I spent one hundred years researching my family's ancestors and could find no evidence of any connection to the Van Helsings," she said. "It was all for nothing, and I can assure you, becoming a vampire was *not* a gift."

My breath caught in my throat as I thought of Mama and the Duke, of how they fought for their rights and longed to walk with humans. They liked being vampires. I mean, I thought they did. *I* liked that they were vampires.

"You don't like being a vampire?" I asked. She'd never even hinted that she might feel that way. "I'm . . . I'm sorry."

"I like being a vampire *now*. I have a family, and the government insists I attend school so that I'll always have friends my own age. Like you. But back then? No. I didn't like it. I was alone, without anyone to help me fit into this world or learn about all this new technology. And don't be sorry. The Council caught and executed Asger for his crime. It's against the code—illegal, I suppose—to turn a human child

28

into one of them. Though enough child vampires exist in the world to prove that many of our kind didn't always care much about code or law." With a shrug, Delphine jerked her chin. "Signal changed. Let's go."

Delphine stepped into the street with confidence, and I hurried along after her.

"And of course, Sophie, things are different now. Vampires lived in the dark, surviving any way we could when y'all thought a white horse wandering a graveyard in the middle of the day meant a vampire lived nearby. That always ended with a letter sent to the Van Helsings, and a vampire hunt was ordered. Nonsense, of course. But I like my life now, especially with the sense of almost-normal. That's why I'm determined to get to the bottom of this. Nobody— not the FBVA, not Asger—will ever have a say in what I do with my life. Just like your birth mom has no say in your life unless you let her. Though if it were me...I'd give anything for five more minutes with my dear mama. I know you love your mothers and all this petition talk is for them, but think about it, okay? Don't do anything you might regret when you're older, because there might come a day when you want Tara Washington in your life. It's all right to want both things."

I nodded. But it wasn't the same. Delphine *knew* her birth mom. I'd never known mine. Not really. She gave me up for adoption when I was eight months old, and until my moms came along, I was in foster care.

As we stepped onto the opposite curb, I reached out to touch her arm.

"I'll think about it. And as for the petition, just give me a month," I said. "That's all. If it doesn't work, we'll come up with a new plan. I promise."

Preferably something that didn't involve talking to internet strangers.

Delphine smiled and linked her arm with mine as we strolled under the huge shopping plaza sign. "If I'm honest, I prefer your plan . . . for now. Diplomacy. A statement."

"Thank you."

"You're welcome. Now, enough dillydallying. We had better pick up our orders before the Duke calls that cellular device of yours. I swear, your mothers don't trust me to see you safe."

That wasn't true at all. They were super happy that I had Delphine in my life. It was hard to make friends when your parents were vampires. Plus... I don't know. Even though there were other kids at school with vampire parents, I felt more at ease with Delphine.

"Come on." Laughing, I sped up as my phone pinged—right on time.

I pulled it from my pocket and swiped the screen.

> Be there in fifteen minutes.
> Love, Mom.

I smiled. The Duke was trying this new thing where she wanted to be called "Mom."

But she would always be my Duke.

Just like Delphine would always be my friend.

Chapter 4

The blood bank was quiet. Almost empty.

My eyes took a second to adjust when we stepped inside, even though the lobby was painted pale blue and lit with bright fluorescent lights. Super modern and clean and medical. But I still had sunbursts in my vision as I got in line at the pickup window.

There was just one person ahead of us. Pretty sure it was the dad of one of the kids in the grade below me. I'd been introduced to him at one of the Hopetown Vampire Society meetings—a kind of local club for vampires and their human families. He was an older vampire Mama had known from her time in Europe. I thought maybe his name was Robert.

Normally, the lobby was packed with humans, sitting in worn black leather chairs and flipping through months-old magazines as they waited to sell their blood—especially on a Saturday. Since vampires went public, the government paid humans a couple hundred bucks for selling one pint every month and a half. Unless you were related to a vampire. That became illegal when vamps started going rogue. Some scientists thought maybe tasting their family's blood triggered them to attack or something.

"Where is everyone?" I mumbled, turning toward Delphine. She shrugged, but her brows were pulled tight above the bridge of her nose. She sort of looked like Mr. Wibbles—my first grade classroom's pet gerbil—when she made that face. But she'd never speak to me again if I told her.

"Oh, good afternoon, Miss Dawes. Miss Abernathy."

Delphine and I turned at the same time Mama's friend noticed us.

"Why, hello there, Mr. De Bourbon." Delphine bobbed a little curtsy.

"A fine day for a stroll, ladies." He smiled a little, looking no older than my moms with his close-cropped hairstyle and magazine-ready clothes. He held a brown paper bag close to his chest, filled with blood bags, no doubt. "Reminds me of winter in N'awlins, Miss Abernathy. One of my favorite cities over the centuries."

Delphine nodded, but I almost laughed when she pressed her lips together. No one from New Orleans really said N'awlins. Mr. De Bourbon glanced at me. "And you, Miss Dawes. How is your dear mama?"

"Good, thank you," I said.

"Please, send her my warmest regards. To your other mama as well."

With a little bow, Mr. De Bourbon strode for the door, and Delphine rolled her eyes.

"I despise that man's airs, Sophie."

Whatever an "air" was. She probably meant his fake Southern drawl. Because it *was* fake.

"Next!"

Startled, I turned, a smile ready for Lisa, the technician.

"Hey, Sophie." Wearing a white medical coat,

with the SynCorps logo stamped on it, Lisa leaned over the counter a little. "How you doing?"

"Okay. Just here to pick up Mama's order." I stepped up to the counter, and Delphine followed.

"That was some game last week, right?" Lisa asked, her fingers flying over the keyboard. "Go Hyenas!"

The Hyenas were Hopetown Middle School's crappy baseball team, but Lisa's nephew was the shortstop, and we all went to the same school, which meant I had to at least act interested.

"Yeah. Heard we lost by only two runs."

"It was amazing," she gushed, making eye contact with me as she hit ENTER. I never needed to give her my name and approved picker-upper number. I collected our order so often she had it memorized. "I think it's going to be a good season. You know Hunter, right? The shortstop?"

Yes, I knew Hunter. No, we didn't hang out. No, I would never tell him Auntie Lisa said hi. Hunter Mulvaney was a Class-A butthead. Always was. Always would be.

He used to call me a vamp-lamp. I didn't even know what that was, but he meant it in a mean way.

"Sure do," I replied, keeping the smile plastered on my face.

Beside me, Delphine grunted—very unladylike of her.

"Oh, hang on," Lisa said, pursing her lips as she glanced at her screen. "Says here the Daweses' order had to be modified due to supply issues, Sophie. I hope that's all right. It seems there's one bag of organic human blood, but the rest is synthetic."

Crap. I bit my lip as Delphine tutted.

"When will y'all be restocked?" Delphine asked, leaning over the counter.

"Umm..." Lisa's fingers flew over the keyboard again. "Maybe the third of next month?"

"The *third*? Of next *month*?" Delphine looked like she might hop over the counter to see whatever popped up on Lisa's screen for herself.

Mama wouldn't be happy with synthetic blood. We were an organic house. Even the Duke said she could smell the chemicals, and Mama refused to let either of them taste it.

"I'm so sorry." With a sigh, Lisa glanced over her shoulder at the refrigerators containing other vampires' orders. "Since that state policy was passed, we haven't seen as many donors as normal."

"What policy?" Delphine asked. Good question. I hadn't heard of any new policy.

"SynCorps is no longer paying for human blood because the governor needs to reroute that money to the FBVA, what with all the rogue cases lately. Testing, doctors. That kind of thing. Anyway, they've been trying to get it approved for over a year, and it finally went into effect last Monday. Unfortunately, that means we're relying on donations to keep up with demand, and we haven't had many volunteers. People aren't always *that* generous." Walking to the nearest refrigerator, Lisa grabbed Mama's "order" and brought it back to the counter. "I'll see if I can get some organic shipped in, girls. I'm so sorry."

"I can't be expected to eat synthetic blood." Delphine pressed her hand to her chest, eyes widening as her mouth hung open. But at least Delphine was talking to me, and not *at* Lisa. "I've never even tasted it."

"According to corporate, this is a new formula. Tastes better, apparently. But I can check to see if I can get organic for you. Abernathy, right?"

"Yes please. I would be much obliged." With a nod, Delphine started fanning herself with her hand. "Sophie, I might need smelling salts. Thank goodness I picked up my order last week."

I rolled my eyes. I had no idea what smelling salts were, but it sounded dramatic.

"Thanks, Lisa. We appreciate it," I said.

"There's a bit of a waiting list. But I just added both your families. Apologize to your moms for me, Sophie. I really hope the blood drive we've organized for next weekend might inspire some people to do the right thing."

"Madam, do you have marketing for this event?" Delphine asked.

With a small smile, Lisa reached beneath the counter and pulled out a handful of flyers. "Sure do. Had a ton of these printed. I don't suppose you'd like to post some at school so the kids can tell their parents about it?"

"It can't hurt," I said with a shrug, taking the flyers as Lisa offered them.

"What does this mean, here. At the bottom?" Delphine asked.

I looked where she pointed.

A+ AND B+ DONORS ONLY AT THIS TIME.

"That's just letting people know it's for vampire use. They're the most common blood types. Rare and O blood types get sent to the hospital." Printing a label, Lisa quickly stuck it onto my bag. "Have to let people know where the blood is going."

"Let me guess." Delphine gave a little snort. "Part of that new policy?"

"Exactly. Sign there, Sophie."

Grabbing the electronic pen, I signed the pin pad for the order.

"Establishments like these already have enough difficulty finding medical blood donors as it is. Syn-Corps is hoping people will just donate for vampires out of the goodness of their hearts?" It was a question, but I knew Delphine well enough to know it wasn't meant to be answered.

Lisa must have realized it too.

A hush fell over the lobby as Lisa pressed her lips together. The only sound was the crinkle of the bag as I grabbed it.

"I really, really hope so, girls," Lisa said at last.

I really hoped so too.

Chapter 5

I was right. Mama was *not* happy. Me and the Duke spent all Saturday evening, and most of Sunday, hearing her complain. She even called the blood bank to give Lisa a piece of her mind.

I locked myself away, listening to music and reading the new graphic novel I bought the week before—a fantasy that was made into a TV show.

"Morning, kiddo." The Duke looked up from her copy of the *New York Times* as I walked into the dining room for breakfast Monday morning. "Chip off the ole block today, eh? Whatcha wearin'?"

Umm. I glanced down at my outfit. Striped, long-sleeve tee, band shirt over it, striped tights, and a knee-length black skirt. Not too out there. I raised a brow.

"Since when do you listen to Metallica?" she asked, turning her attention back to the paper. Probably the stocks page—she loved those stocks. "Must be thirty years since I first saw them in concert, and still my favorite."

"Oh," I said, sitting next to her. Mama had outdone herself. Scrambled eggs, bacon, pork roll, toast, and three different flavors of jelly. It was hard to screw up bacon . . . but I'd need salt for the poor eggs. They looked a little brown. "Are they a band? I just saw it at the store and thought it looked cute."

"Cute." The Duke snorted and looked at me over the paper. "Metallica are gods, kiddo."

I chuckled and eyed my plate. Maybe eggs first, then down it with bacon? Or . . . both together?

"Bacon first," whispered the Duke, leaning toward me. "We didn't have bacon when I was growing up, but we did have salted pork. Should cover the taste the same."

Solid plan. I dug in, and the Duke smiled. "Five minutes, then we've got to get moving."

I glanced at her. She was dressed for the boardroom—tailored black blazer, deep blue silk blouse, tailored calf-length skirt, six-inch heels, and—what I called—battle braids.

The Duke was a Viking way back—a shield-maiden warrior—and any time she had to tackle the board of directors, she twisted her long white-blond hair into four tight French braids that met in one big braid at the back of her head.

"You got it," I replied, downing half a glass of orange juice. The eggs weren't just a little brown, they were burnt.

"Morning, *ma petite*." Mama entered the dining room, wearing her typical fifties housewife chic and a bright smile. "Look at you, Freyja."

The Duke startled and looked up. Mama didn't use her name often. It was always the Duke, or darling, or dear. I was surprised too, and turned, fork halfway to my mouth, to stare at Mama.

"What? What is it?" The Duke asked, putting down the paper before grabbing a napkin. We must've had the same thought. Maybe her suit was dirty? It was important to both my moms to look as perfect as possible so no humans would be all "if they leave the house like that, imagine the mess their kid lives in." No dirt, no smudges, clothes ironed. Healthy, happy, smiling at all times—so no one made a "concerned" call to CPS.

"That color." Mama smiled even wider as she sat next to the Duke. "Do you remember? You wore that same color the night you fought a duel in my honor. It was the night we first met. Versailles, remember?"

The Duke's perfectly manicured blond brows knitted together, so Mama looked at me.

"She was amazing, Sophie," Mama gushed. "We all knew her as the Duke of Anjou—she was masquerading as a man."

That much, I knew.

"Well, a horrible noble had insisted on peeking at my stockinged ankles—a scandal at the time— and the great, deadly Duke of Anjou swooped in to challenge him to a duel. She wore a beautiful suit of that exact shade of dark blue, with silver flowers embroidered into it."

"Deadly?" I asked, my lips quirking into a smile as I glanced at the Duke.

"It was another time." With a shrug, the Duke leaned toward Mama and placed a gentle kiss against her cheek. They were so gross. "Of course, I remember. And you were the loveliest of all the court ladies."

Mama blushed, and I grabbed a piece of toast as I stood. "We're going to be late, Mama."

"Go, go," she shooed, sitting back. "You both have a wonderful day. I'm making meatballs for dinner, Sophie."

"She can't wait, I'm sure." The Duke shared a secret smile with me as she pushed to her feet. "And for us, my love? A perfectly heated B-negative, I hope?"

"Gah." The disgusted scoff scraped from the very back of Mama's throat. "We finished all the organic blood yesterday, so we're stuck with that synthetic swill."

"No matter." Stepping close to Mama, the Duke kissed her forehead. "With your care, it will be delicious."

"Thank you," Mama said with a sigh, before turning to me. "Your lunch is on the counter."

"Thanks, Mama." Darn it.

In the brand-new Mercedes, the Duke fiddled with the music controls as we drove.

"What's this?" I asked, as electric guitars blared from the speakers.

"Metallica. And, you're welcome." Pretending the steering wheel was a drum kit, she lashed it in time with the percussion.

I laughed, and she reached into the center console.

"Here, kiddo." Ten bucks. Sweet. "For lunch. I'll have another talk with her tonight. You should at least be able to make your own lunch."

"Thanks, Mom."

The Duke smiled and glanced at me. "She means well."

"I know she does."

"And she tries very hard. All she wants is to be the perfect mom for you. Me too."

I smiled.

School was only a few blocks away, but the Duke insisted on driving me every day. She said it was so we had some quality time together. Whatever the reason, I liked it.

It was another warm, sunny day, and as we pulled into the car line at school, I saw a lot of the kids wore tees and shorts. Glancing at my striped sleeves, I shrugged. It's not like I usually fit in anyway.

Hopetown Middle School matched the rest of the town, with a brick exterior to make it look like it'd been there forever. It was kind of pretty, with its well-kept lawn and trees planted at perfect intervals.

"Hmm." The Duke leaned over the steering wheel and squinted. The car line wasn't moving.

That's when I saw the red and blue lights.

"Cops?" I asked.

"Darn it," she murmured. "No. FBVA."

It wasn't what she said, but how she said it. My heart dropped into my stomach. FBVA at school, plus that reaction, meant only one thing.

"Was there another attack?"

I watched as she pursed her lips and nodded.

Crap. That meant there would be an assembly, with Principal Forrester looking all stern as he stared at all the kids of vampires in the bleachers—just in case we were in on some kind of vampires-going-rogue conspiracy.

Worst Monday ever.

"Don't worry, kiddo." With a sigh, the Duke turned and planted a kiss on my cheek. "Just do your schoolwork and everything will be fine."

"You have your ID?" I asked. The FBVA were probably checking all drivers as they left the car line.

"Don't worry about me. Worry about your grades." The Duke smiled and reached into the back seat to grab my bag. "Odin's eye, that's heavy. Whaddya have in there?"

"Math."

"Math." With a snort, she handed it over. "Hey, kiddo."

I glanced at her expectantly, placing the strap over my shoulder.

"I love you."

"Love you too, Mom." I wanted to say *be safe*, but I knew she would be.

No one messed with Freyja Knutsdatter Dawes.

Not anyone in the last 1,200 years.

Chapter 6

No doubt some of you may have heard there was an incident last night. Unfortunately, it was local. As this is Hopetown's first rogue case, the town will be sending patrol cars onto the streets to ensure human safety." A murmur rolled through the packed gym as Mr. Forrester spoke.

But I sat frozen like a statue. Local? Had the Duke known?

"We will be sending literature home to all your parents today. Some tips and tricks to keep your families safe in the event that you find yourselves victims of a rogue attack." Mr. Forrester lifted a pamphlet into the air, and my chest tightened as a few of the kids shot wary glances over their shoulders. At me. At Delphine. At the other kids of vampires.

They were scared, but so were we. And now they were scared of us.

I scowled at Mr. Forrester. On his left stood the vice principal, the vampire-student relations officer, and all the teachers. FBVA officers stood off to the right. But behind them, painted on the wall, was the Hopetown Hyenas mural—all dark blue and white with a splash of gold, the hyena looking more like a big cat mid-roar as it burst through the *A*. Ready to attack. It screamed "danger," just like Mr. Forrester screamed "danger" right now. I didn't like it.

"We'll be joining the fine officers of the FBVA in a demonstration that might save your life," he continued. "Until we know what causes this . . . illness, we must all use caution."

"This is ridiculous," Delphine whispered.

"Our thoughts and prayers go out to the De Bourbon family, and we hope they are returned to us soon." Mr. Forrester glanced around the gym. "Counselors will be available to anyone who needs one. Whether you know a family member, or feel personally affected, we're all in this together."

"Oh my goodness," Delphine breathed, placing a cold hand over mine. I doubted there was another De Bourbon family in Hopetown, and that meant Mama's friend—the one we ran into at the blood bank—went rogue.

My stomach went all fluttery, and I swallowed the lump that formed in my throat as one of the FBVA agents stepped up to the mic.

They showed us some basic self-defense moves. Even had us all stand to practice after the teachers role-played attacker versus victim.

The assembly ended on a brighter note, when the vampire-student relations officer took the mic to remind everyone—teachers included—that vampires weren't dangerous. That something unknown caused the rogue phenomenon, and that we had to come together as a community to help one another.

Mr. Forrester frowned and most of the students whispered to one another, but it made me feel a little better.

Because I *knew* my moms wouldn't just go

attacking people, even if humans didn't fully trust them. Neither would Delphine. And we'd all get through this if we just worked with one another. Vampires and humans together.

That's why the petition to the governor had to work.

Which was what I kept telling myself throughout the assembly and all the way to the cafeteria for lunch.

"Do they really think a jab to the ribs will help in a dangerous situation like that?" Delphine asked, sipping blood from her pink-and-purple thermos covered with cartoon ponies. We sat next to each other at one of the round, white cafeteria tables. Alone. Normally, our table was packed with new faces every day—some talking to us, some not. But not today. It was like they thought Delphine was going to go rogue right there at lunch. "It's ridiculous, really. I can take down full-grown men. How do they think we ate before walking into the light?"

"I dunno, D." But I did know she was right. A kid was no match for an adult human, never mind a rogue vampire with all their regular super-vampire strength kicked up twenty notches by whatever drove them wild. It gave me the shivers.

"They're trying to get everyone killed with these assemblies. Best thing anyone can do is travel in pairs, and run. Fifty-fifty chance. Someone's always going to be slower."

"Delphine." I used my best Mama voice. She was being really loud, and the cafeteria was unusually quiet.

"No need to take that tone with me, Sophie Dawes," Delphine said, rolling her eyes. "You know I'm right. And if Mr. Forrester hadn't made it sound like we're all bloodthirsty monsters, we'd have a full lunch table, and I could warn them."

"Run and hope for the best though?" My lips twitched with amusement. She was right, of course. The Duke had given me the same advice, but that wasn't the point. "People are scared."

"*Vampires* are scared." With a sigh, she took a long sip of her blood lunch. "In all my history, this has never happened. Are there bad vampires out there? Yes. But to have no control? To attack the very humans we've wanted to live beside for *centuries*?

Absolutely not. If the school truly cared for student safety, they'd provide everyone with potent garlic spray. Spritz and run. That would increase everyone's survival."

I smiled. There was one major problem with that. The kind of garlic spray that could knock out a vampire had to soak in oak barrels for two hundred years to make it super strong. It was rare. Mainly because two hundred years ago, no one knew vampires would be in the light, or going rogue, so no one thought to make enough barrels of it to protect all humans. Regular garlic, or garlic oil, just made a vampire's eyes water.

Luckily, we had some in our "rogue kit" at home—a big bulky box of emergency things that would help if a rogue vampire ever got into our house.

"Then there's the extra abilities," Delphine continued. "If rogue vampires lose control, what good is a jab to the ribs if they can still glamour the victim?"

My eyebrows arched. I hadn't even thought of that. Some vampires were able to calm their victims by using a kind of mind control called glamour. Others could turn themselves into animals to avoid people noticing them. There were even some who could turn themselves invisible. But when vampires walked into the light, they promised to never use those extra powers again. It was all illegal now.

"You mean, they'd just use it because it's part of them?"

"Exactly!"

My phone buzzed in my pocket, and I fished it out. It was a text from the Duke.

How was the assembly? Are you OK? How's Delphine?

Sighing, I thumbed a quick response.

I'm OK. Assembly was weird.

"Who's that?" Delphine asked, taking another sip from her thermos.

"The Duke. She's just making sure we're okay."

"I swear, your mamas are simply the best."

They really were. My phone buzzed again.

It was an old friend of Mama's.
Make sure you go straight home.
No detours. Same with Delphine.
Mama says the police came to
ask a few routine questions.

My eyebrows scrunched together. **Why?** I texted.

"Everything all right?" Delphine asked.

"Yeah . . . she says to go straight home." My phone
buzzed.

He didn't just go rogue. He killed
someone. Please be safe.

Chapter 7

The Duke's words repeated in my head all through the rest of my classes. Even Delphine was quiet, which was weird. I expected her to make another case for contacting Anon715 to find out what they knew, but she didn't. It was like going rogue was some far-off distant thing that wouldn't happen to my family. Something that happened in other places. Not here in Hopetown.

Before, I worried that the constant CPS visits might make my moms give me up—even after living with them for five years, and *especially* when my birth mom contacted us. But now I knew Delphine was right. Going rogue was the real danger.

As I walked home, bright sun shining despite the storm cloud hanging over my thoughts, all I could think about was my family. My moms. How happy we were. How much we loved one another. And how I hoped going rogue would never touch my family. The Duke was 1,200 years old. She said the older the vampire, the more powerful. The more control. And Mama? Mama was too sweet and gentle. She was so sweet and gentle, I always wondered how she survived before vampires walked into the light. There's no way she'd be able to hurt anyone, even to eat. Even if she was starving.

Like I was starving that very moment. I hurried home, stomach gurgling as I jogged up the familiar cobblestone drive nestled between two narrow, manicured lawns—a really nice contrast against our lovely white house with black-painted windowsills— and turned the key in the front door.

I dropped my bag on the stairs and went into the kitchen to grab an apple before homework. But as I entered the kitchen, I paused and smiled. There was Mama, dancing around the island. She had something super poppy on the speakers, twirling from stove to island and back, sprinkling love and herbs into whatever disaster she was making.

"Hi, Mama," I called, grabbing an apple from the basket at the edge of the countertop.

She whirled, a hand to her chest. I scared her. "*Mon dieu*, Sophie!"

"Your super-hearing is getting rusty." Smiling, I stepped around the island and gave her a tight hug. She froze a little at first, probably surprised, but something had tugged at my heart when I saw her. Dancing. Cooking. Always there for me, always trying to be the best mom in the world.

Mama was cold to the touch—she always was—but I ran hot enough for both of us, and she melted into my hug.

"Baby." She nuzzled the top of my head with her cheek and stroked the back of my neck. "You had a rough day."

Not as rough as her. "The Duke texted me about the police. I'm sorry about Mr. De Bourbon."

"It was all very routine: They asked the last time I saw him, who might know something. That kind of thing," she said with a sigh. "I'm so very sorry for him and his family. And the victim, of course."

"I'm sorry too, Mama. I love you."

"Love you too, baby." She pulled away from me a little and searched my face. "Are you sure you're okay? If you need to talk to someone, you can talk to me."

"Thank you, but I'm all right." I cleared my throat and took a step backward. I wasn't all right. Not really. But I didn't want to offload my feelings after the day Mama had. Her friend was gone, not mine.

"All right. Do your homework. Dinner will be at six thirty. The Duke's running late."

"You got it," I replied, taking a big bite out of the apple. She scowled, and I smiled. "Sophie Anne Dawes. If you ruin your dinner—"

"I won't, Mama." I turned on my heel and made for the door. "Promise."

That's when I noticed the doll sitting next to the cereal on the counter. It was the same one Laura had noticed. Mama's new one.

"What's up with the doll?" I asked, and Mama turned to point at it.

"I was cleaning her a little. Poor *belle* needed some new paint. She looks good, no?"

She meant "right," but it was still a big no from me.

It was creepy. The doll wore a dress fitted with long, narrow sleeves, then the skirt sharply jutted out at the waist, draping over a super-wide cage worn beneath. I knew people used to wear dresses like that. Mama told awesome stories about her time as Marie Antoinette's best friend back in the 1700s, but I had no idea how anyone walked through doors wearing them. The skirts were too wide. And the doll's face was cracked, its white hair piled high and held in place with peeling glue and a raggedy, tiny, fake ostrich feather.

"Sure, Mama," I said, raising an eyebrow. "Great job."

"Six thirty!" she reminded me, turning back to what she was doing.

I looked at the doll one last time, and left the room.

Math. Social studies. Reading.

My head swam with numbers and countries and protons in between bouts of shallow breaths and wondering if dinner was going to turn into a big serious talk about what the arrival of "going rogue" in Hopetown meant for our family.

Glancing at my plain white desk, I sighed. I still had to read a chapter of *Brown Girl Dreaming*, but concentrating was pointless, and it was almost six thirty anyway. I'd try to read later, at bedtime. When dinner was over and I could really let myself get swept away by the story.

With a groan, I stood and stretched. All I wanted were my pajamas, but Mama would be upset if I didn't come to dinner dressed.

We always "dressed" for dinner. Mama would change into an old-timey evening gown, decked in jewels with her hair piled high. And the Duke would slip into tuxedo tails with a long flowy skirt, complete with top hat, cane, and black leather gloves.

As for me, I had a few frilly dresses Mama had

bought—that I hated—but it was tradition, so I went with it.

The Duke hated it too. She said the hundreds of years between the plague and the 1970s sucked, and she'd prefer to relax after a long day's work.

Same. Seriously.

Right. I quickly undressed and chose the least frilly dress from my closet. It was pink—of course—but the skirt part went straight down, and a pretty layer of lace covered the silky fabric. I could probably pull my hair up with a few clips to the side of my head. That should be enough. I wasn't in the mood to spend a lot of time on it.

With a sigh, I bent to grab the accessory container from under my bed, and frowned as my eyes slid to the *other* box. The purple one with the word PRIVATE written on it in silver glitter. Where I'd put the letter from my birth mom.

That was a habit I didn't think I'd ever get rid of—labeling things as "private." I'd been really lucky as a baby and was fostered out with this nice family, who were able to give me a home until I was six. I think they probably would have adopted me, because they had no other kids—fostered or biological—but Mr. Hoff got a new job overseas, and the state wouldn't let me go with them. Sometimes I missed them, but Mr. and Mrs. Hoff still sent me birthday cards and gifts.

Then there was Mr. and Mrs. Galbretti—my second set of foster parents—who I hadn't heard from since I left their care. They were kind, but the house was so loud and busy. The constant chaos made me worried and anxious, but I was barely there a year before my moms swooped in and adopted me. The Galbrettis had two biological kids of their own, and five other foster kids, not including me. And *that's* when I learned to label things as "private." My shoes, my coat, my socks, my box of memories, and important things.

I frowned. I guess a letter from my birth mom *was* an "important thing."

But that was the last thing I needed to think about right now.

I shook my head, pulled out the accessory container, and sat on the bed.

Pins, scrunchies, clips.

Plenty of pink to match the dress—thanks, Mama.

"Knock, knock?" The call was followed by an actual knock before the door opened, and the Duke popped her head in. When she saw me, she rolled her eyes. "That's not your color."

"No kidding." I smiled a little as she entered the room. Her hair was still braided the same way from that morning, but she wore her usual dinner outfit.

"Ready?" she asked.

"Yeah. Let me just..." I grabbed two clips from my dresser and quickly pulled up my hair. I must've completely spaced out. Mama normally called up the stairs when the Duke got home so I knew to get ready. "I didn't know you were home."

"Got in about thirty minutes ago." She pressed a kiss to my temple as I walked up to her, and all the weird stuff from the assembly came flooding back. If anyone could help me by talking about how I didn't feel the school was on our side, it would be the Duke. She was really calm, and steady, and wouldn't pry if things got heavy...but when I glanced up at her face, she seemed distracted. "I could really use a fine bag of B-negative tonight. It was a rough day."

I swallowed. It could wait until tomorrow. And now I felt bad, because there was no B-negative for dinner, only that synthetic stuff.

"Come on, kiddo." With a tired smile, she held out her arm like they did in old movies, and I linked my arm with hers. "Let's see what Mama rustled up for your dinner.... Hope you ate double at lunch."

We joked around as we left my room and walked down the stairs. About her day—and the board members not liking when the Duke took charge of things. About how she negotiated a deal that would put her company on the Fortune 500 list.

And as we entered the dim-lit dining room—ambience, Mama called it—I felt a little lighter. A bit less sad, and some of the sickness in my belly had disappeared.

Until I saw Mama. Pursing my lips, I tilted my head to the side.

Her back was to us as she stared out the dining room window, but that in itself wasn't weird. What was weird was that she hadn't changed her clothes. She wore the same outfit as before—her housewife garb. And in her right hand was her new porcelain doll, except its head was missing.

"Mama?" The little hairs on my arms rose as I stared at the doll. "What happened?"

But she didn't answer.

"Marie?" The Duke sounded as confused as I was. "Do you want a few minutes to get ready?"

Dinner was on the perfectly set table. Burnt bread, pan-scraped Bolognese, and three different kinds of overcooked, mushy pasta in case I didn't want spaghetti. In front of my chair was an empty plate made of fine china, with three forks on one side, two knives on the other. The Duke's crystal goblet, filled with blood, sat on top of another fine china plate.

And that's when I noticed Mama's goblet. She started without us. Her blood was half-gone.

"Marie?" The Duke asked, taking another step into the room. She sniffed the air, and I froze. "Marie? What is it?"

That's when I heard it. It sounded like a growl.

The kind a sick or injured dog makes when a person gets too close to it. All low and grumbly. My palms went slippery as the sound made all the hair on my body stand up.

"Sophie." The Duke didn't move as she spoke, but her voice was low and even. "I need you to back up very slowly and go upstairs. Do you understand?"

No, I didn't understand. And my heart began to drum a little too fast. A little too frantic. "Yes."

"Lock the door to your room," she said, taking a slow, measured step forward. "And do not come out, no matter what you hear."

This day really couldn't get this much worse... could it? Mama probably had a bee in her bonnet about something. That's all. Something had happened, and the Duke would calm her down and we could get back to dinner like nothing had happened.

But then Mama turned, and all the blood in my body drained to my toes. I felt dizzy, like I might faint.

Mama's eyes were full red, and her fangs were all the way out of her mouth, like they were when vampires drank fresh blood, straight from humans. Her fangs glistened in the dim distance, catching what little light there was. I stared, my brain telling me to do what the Duke had told me, but my feet wouldn't listen.

And that's when her bloodred eyes locked onto mine, and her lips curled back into a weird, creepy smile as her fangs snapped down even more.

"Sophie." The Duke repeated, but this time her voice was hard as she stepped directly in front of me, not turning, never taking her eyes off Mama. "Run, Sophie."

My eyes burned as my body pieced everything together faster than my brain could manage.

Run. Yes. Absolutely.

Mama—my sweet, loving mama—was going rogue.

Chapter 8

I bolted from the room.

This couldn't be happening. No way. No how.

And there wasn't a hope in Hopetown, Pennsylvania, that I was going to run upstairs and lock myself in my room. Not even as an earsplitting screech sounded from the dining room, followed by the shattering of glass. I clapped my hands over my ears and skidded to a stop at the foot of the stairs.

Think. Calm.

First, if the Duke couldn't get Mama under control, Mama would bust down my bedroom door... and I wasn't sure I'd be okay if I jumped out the window. Broken bones. Sprains. Then I'd be a sitting duck. Delphine was right. A jab to the ribs wouldn't work, and running was useless.

Second, I knew where the rogue emergency kit was, and it sure as heck wasn't in my bedroom.

Third, if we wanted to stop Mama from leaving the house, the Duke would need that emergency kit.

I lowered my hands from my ears, arms shaking as my chest tightened, making it hard to breathe.

If Mama left the house, she might attack someone, and the FBVA would be called. That was the whole point of having an emergency kit—to keep a rogue parent from leaving. It wasn't just to protect me, it was to protect our family. If we could hide that one of them went rogue, then the FBVA wouldn't be notified, and couldn't take us to the facility.

And that meant I had to suck it up. I had to breathe in. And out.

Another crash thundered from the dining room, and an angry scream sent a chill up my spine.

The office. The kit was in the Duke's office.

Heart pounding, I pivoted away from the stairs

and ran down the window-lined hallway that led to the downstairs bathroom, and the Duke's office.

Night had fallen.

Running in the dark, I almost tripped over the white wicker chair where Mama liked to sit and craft. She loved to sit in the light as she stabbed an embroidery needle through fabric...all while wearing a ridiculously large sun hat.

She always smelled of sun and strawberries, ready with hugs and kisses.

And as I passed the chair, then the living room, then bathroom, I had to swipe a forearm over my face to get rid of the silly tears.

Everything would be okay.

I practically slammed into the office door as the sound of my parents' struggle spilled beyond the dining room. More glass shattered. Furniture turned over.

And I grabbed the door handle with sweaty palms.

Eyes wide, I scanned the room. It was dark, but I didn't want to turn on the light. Like, in the dark

I could pretend it was a nightmare, and as soon as I grabbed the kit everything would go back to normal.

It was a big office. The Duke's desk was large enough to have two computer screens and two phone lines. Behind me, mounted on the wall next to the door was a huge TV screen she used for video conferences, and below it, a hard leather couch.

Everywhere I turned were memories. Things I didn't even think about, like sitting on that hard couch, reading books when the Duke had to work on the weekends, with Mama in her wicker chair in the hall, humming. Or the times when we'd all come down here to watch an action movie on the big flat-screen—to pretend we were at the movies—with popcorn and blankets, and enough soda to keep me up way too late. But all that would be taken away if Mama got out of the house.

Third filing cabinet on the left. Bottom drawer. Unlocked. Always unlocked. I knew where everything was and how to get to it. The Duke insisted that we do emergency drills, just in case.

Heart pounding, I ran to the wall of filing cabinets, skimming my hands over the metal until I found the third row, then dropped down to grab the handle of the bottom drawer.

It was there—a big black shoebox. I knew what was inside. Things meant to contain, not hurt . . . too much:

A mason jar of brick dust. That was to make a circle around the rogue vampire. Once it was on the ground, the vampire couldn't walk across its boundary.

A bottle of tar water, not holy water. Tar water created a protective barrier that prevented vampires from entering an area—like a human home—without an invitation.

A small, handheld crossbow with eight rounds of small wooden arrows. Wood can hurt a vampire, but not really kill one.

A coil of silver rope, soaked in garlic oil, to restrain a vampire.

And a spray bottle filled with trusty garlic oil, to stun.

My heartbeat made me dizzy as I left the office and ran down the hall.

Passing Mama's white wicker chair, I winced at

73

the sound of more breaking glass. It seemed farther away...maybe back in the living room? I turned the corner, stairs to my right, and ahead...a war zone. The little table by the front door was destroyed, its legs broken off with large jagged splinters scattered everywhere. The house phone was pulled from the wall, its base by the door, the handset...who knew?

A layer of shattered glass glittered in the hall, moonlight from the windowpanes in the front door melting into the soft yellow glow of the dimmed dining room lights.

I swallowed and crouched to open the emergency kit.

Tar water, brick dust, crossbow—all there. But that was for later.

A snarly growl, a really loud snarly growl, stopped me dead. The hair on the back of my neck stood on end, and goose bumps rolled over my bare arms. It definitely came from the dining room.

There was a crunch. And another. Then slow, methodical footsteps followed by low murmurs.

Time was up. One or both of my moms were tiring, and that meant I had to act. Now.

I turned my attention back to the box and nudged the rope to the side.

There it was. The spray bottle.

I grabbed it and stood, leaving the box on the floor.

Quiet. I had to be quiet, but the darn glass made that really hard. *Crunch*. I winced, but kept on crunching, as carefully as I could, my hand squeezing the spray bottle so hard I thought I might bend the plastic.

Until I was there. At the door. Ready to peek around the corner.

Breathing deep, I took a half step and peered around the destroyed dining room. Broken chairs and vases. Plates smashed. Furniture flipped over. Even worse . . . Mama's doll collection was destroyed, heads and bodies smashed, their dresses ripped and ruined.

But nothing prepared me for my moms.

They were covered in blood, and my heart stuck in my throat. The Duke murmured softly, hands out, calming, while Mama babbled in French, angry, excited.

They circled each other, stepping over broken pieces of pottery and glass, but then the Duke saw me. Her eyes widened, then slid to the spray bottle. She nodded and gestured with her right hand. Thank goodness she still wore her black leather gloves. They would protect her skin.

A lump formed in my throat, but I forced it down. Way down. Before tossing the spray bottle—filled with garlic oil—across the room.

I watched as the Duke caught the bottle, swooping it from the air like the swords of her shield-maiden human days.

As she took aim, pulling the lapel of her coat over her face to protect herself from the spray, I screwed my eyes shut.

I couldn't watch.

But I heard Mama's screams as the Duke pulled the trigger.

Chapter 9

I sat at the top of the stairs, face smooshed into my hands, smearing salty tears into my hot skin. None of this could be happening. But it was. It was as real as me, or as my parents, or as Delphine's mom, who swept shards of glass at the bottom of the stairs.

The Duke had called in vampire allies for backup.

"You okay up there, Sophie?" Delphine's mom called over the crackly sound of glass hitting the dustpan.

I wasn't sure I'd ever be okay again, honestly. "Yeah."

"What a question, Mom. Sophie's obviously distraught."

I sat up straight as Delphine came into view, a big honking mug of my favorite thing in her hands. Hot chocolate. She wore pajama pants, slippers, and a fuzzy sweater—very un-Delphine. But it was late, and I knew her family would come straight over when the Duke called.

I looked at Delphine. Her eyes were squinted and her lips pressed together as she started up the stairs. I wondered if she was thinking what I was thinking, because if it happened to Mama, it could happen to her. She could be next. Or the Duke.

I shivered.

"I think we're all distraught," Delphine's mom said with a sigh.

"I know, Mom." Delphine's voice went all soft as she sat next to me on the stairs. She glanced down at her mother, whose eyes looked all teary from where we were.

"At least we're nearby to help." Delphine's mom nodded. "You girls just stay up there. I'm going to go check on Daddy and the Duke. I'll be back."

Delphine smiled as her mom gathered the dustpan and strode toward the dining room, then turned to me. "Here, Sophie. Get that in you. I hope I made it right."

"Thanks," I said, carefully taking the hot mug from her hands. I smiled a little, ready to play up the "I'm okay" thing, but as I took a sip of the hot chocolate, my shoulders drooped with the weight of what had happened.

"Hush," Delphine said, hugging my waist. "The Duke knows what she's doing. She'll make this right, I guarantee you that."

It was a really nice thing to say, but they were just words. The Duke could fix lots of things, but she wasn't a vampire doctor, and there wasn't a cure. What was she going to do? Keep Mama locked in the basement until she stopped going rogue? I sipped the hot chocolate, then took a deep, shuddering breath. "Delphine?"

"Yes?"

"I don't want to go to a facility." My voice was almost a whisper, so I cleared my throat. "I don't want to go, and I don't want my moms to go."

"I know, Sophie. Nobody wants that."

It was weird, Delphine's calmness. When things like this happened to other people, she was loud and brash and calling for some sort of revolution. I wanted to scream and yell. I wanted to march down to that basement and demand to know what caused this. Because there had to be a reason. Something or someone I could blame. This was my *family*, and we were hours from disaster. Days, if the Duke could figure out how to keep it quiet.

I took another sip of chocolate, heart pounding so fast I thought it'd burst. I turned to Delphine. We had to do something. Deep down, I knew a petition to the governor wasn't going to fix anything fast enough to help us. It would have to be me. Us. We were going to have to do something ourselves. "Okay."

"Okay?" she asked, both brows arching as she glanced at me. "Okay, what?"

"Let's do it. Let's contact Anon715."

We sat there for a minute, staring at each other. I was serious, and could tell she was trying to figure out if I was kidding.

"I mean it," I said. "We'll contact them, like you wanted, and see what we can find out about this antidote."

"Sophie," she began. But she said my name really slow, like she was going to try and talk me out of it. "You're upset and in shock right now."

Upset didn't begin to cover it, and I was beyond shock. Anger bubbled hot and dangerous just under my skin. "I'm fine, Delphine. Really. But no one is going to help us. The minute someone finds out Mama is tied up in the basement, they're going to shove us into a van and I'll never see you again. There isn't a doctor we can go to. Nothing on the internet. Maybe you're right. Maybe Anon715 has the answers we need."

More silence. She looked away, and my stomach knotted up with that awful dread kind of feeling.

The boiling anger inside turned to a chill as reality froze the blood in my veins. What would happen to Mama? To the Duke? To me? What *happened* when people were taken to that facility?

Something told me the answers wouldn't make me feel better.

"For all we know, the rogue phase passes, Sophie." Delphine's voice was soft, and my heart sank. This was it. The end. She was going to say no. "My concern has always been what happens once vampires and their families are sent to the facility. The whole 'what happens next' thing. I don't really know if we'll be able to find anything to help your mama. Or if we'd be able to find the antidote . . . *if* it even exists."

"I know that. But something went wrong, Delphine. I got home from school, and she was fine. It was like a light switch." I was talking really fast, but I had to convince her. Anon715 had to know *something*. Something we could take to the governor or the press. Something that would change the process. If what the FBVA said was true—that they spent billions on searching for a cure while trying to rehabilitate rogue vamps—there was no need to take whole families. People should be able to visit and see progress. Tears welled in my eyes. "I'm scared, Delphine. I don't want that happening to the Duke or to you."

Another silence. "Sophie. Back when the original

Council first put the idea of stepping into the light before our people, there were many with...feelings. Council members included. We've stood witness to some of your kind's greatest atrocities. Humans can sometimes be nothing more than monsters disguised as righteous lambs. And we knew it wouldn't be easy to fit in, that there would be many who would hate us. And there's no better way to wage war on those viewed as an enemy than to destroy the one thing they can control."

Delphine's voice got raspy and dark as she spoke. But I knew how much the words meant to her by the way she angrily spat them out.

"Do you know what that one thing is?" she asked, eyes locking onto mine.

A shiver ran up my spine as I saw what was behind those eyes. I didn't notice it often, but tonight, in the dim light, sitting at the top of my stairs, there it was. Something old and ancient and not close to twelve years old stared back at me.

A lump formed in my throat, and as I shook my head, I swallowed it down. This was still my friend. But tired. Fed up.

"Perception, Sophie." With a snort, she pointed at herself, then at me. "Do you know how difficult it is to try and never do the wrong thing? We're not allowed, because to live in the light means vampires have to be better than good. And for some of us it's a struggle to keep up the act. Even I struggle from time to time. But the more we're accepted, the greater threat we become in the eyes of those in charge. They know the truth. How powerful we are. Vampires going rogue destroys the happy image we've projected all these years. And the more of us that go rogue, the less we'll be accepted. Fear will drive the people to beg the government to step in. Today, it's rogue vampires and their families. Tomorrow? They'll round up *all* vampires. Makes you wonder what the point of stepping into the light even was. Freedom? Sure. But at what cost? Many of us saw this coming. We just never imagined it would be so soon."

My thoughts flitted to Mama, to how "perfect" she always wanted to be in the eyes of humans. She was on the PTA, a member of the neighborhood flower club. She cooked because that's what human moms did for their families. Mama cleaned every day like the house was a mess, because "What if someone came over?" She kept everything in order. She ran the house like the Duke ran her boardroom. "How could the government have gotten to Mama? Can you threaten someone into going rogue? How does it even work?"

"Vampires have never 'gone rogue.'" Delphine watched as I took another sip of my hot chocolate before continuing. "The only thing that comes close is when a new vampire is turned. For a time, baby vampires need a lot to eat and have trouble controlling their new senses, which can lead to aggression."

"Well, Mama's definitely not new." With a sigh, I took another sip.

"Think, Sophie. Has she had a change in routine? Somewhere new she's started going?"

I shook my head. Nothing had changed. Nothing was different.

"Sophie?" We both stiffened as the Duke called from somewhere in the house.

"Yeah, Mom?" I yelled.

Her steps, normally so light, sounded heavy as she trudged down the hall. It took a minute, but she turned the corner at the bottom of the stairs and looked up.

I didn't like what I saw. Dark circles beneath her eyes deepened the shadows on her face. Her lips were almost as pale as her skin. Her clothes, all messy and torn. The only things still intact were her braids. With only a few flyaways.

"Hey, kiddo." She sounded so small that tears welled in my eyes again. She was my rock. My strong, Viking shield-maiden. My mom. She wasn't allowed to sound small and frightened, because I didn't think I could be a warrior for her.

"Hi," I whispered.

"I think we're mostly cleaned up," she said, glancing at Delphine. "Your parents are leaving, Delphine."

Delphine nodded.

"Sophie, if you'd like, you could spend the night at Delphine's." The Duke looked at me sharply—a no-nonsense, *don't make me fight about this* kind of look—and I immediately understood why.

"I'm not afraid of Mama." But my voice broke midsentence, and the Duke closed her eyes against my lie. "You have everything under control. She's . . ."

Contained. But I couldn't say the word.

"For now."

"Sophie, you should come with us," Delphine said. "It might be too dangerous—"

"It's not," I snapped. "Besides, it's a school night, and people would wonder why."

The Duke nodded.

"I'd prefer if you went with Delphine." But there was no fight left in her. I could tell by the stiffness in her shoulders and the way she leaned on the banister.

"Are you all right, Mom?"

The Duke shook her head but glanced up at me, a weak smile on her face. "Too much excitement on an empty stomach. We never did eat dinner."

As if on cue, my stomach growled.

"Come on, kiddo. Let's say goodbye to our friends. You can whip yourself up a sandwich and I'll head down to the basement and grab a blood bag."

"Basement?" I asked, making a move to stand.

"Yeah." Sighing, the Duke took a step back from the base of the stairs as Delphine started down ahead of me. "That synthetic stuff needs to be kept at a specific temperature, so we put it in the basement refrigerator."

Synthetic...

My eyes widened as I flashed back to dinner. Walking into the dining room. Mama's back to us. One goblet full of blood for the Duke, and Mama's... half-empty.

"No!" The word was out of my mouth before I could stop it, and Delphine whipped around to look at me.

"Sophie? What is it?"

It might not be a change of routine, but the synthetic blood was something new, and so was the new policy that meant more vampires would have to eat synthetic blood and the new formula that made it taste better.

Something my moms had never tried before. Maybe something in it had turned both Mama and Mr. De Bourbon rogue.

My palms went all clammy, and I thought I'd drop the hot chocolate as my eyes met Delphine's.

"Blood," I said.

She raised her brows.

"The blood. It's the synthetic blood!"

Chapter 10

That night I tossed and turned, unable to sleep after everything. Between Mama, the blood, and Delphine's parents offering to donate theirs so the Duke could eat, I was overwhelmed.

Thank goodness the Duke had kept the old medical equipment vampires had needed back when they first walked into the light, before the blood banks stepped in so they didn't have to find their own donors. Delphine's parents were so good to offer, and promised they'd donate again as soon as they could.

The Duke would have to ration it. There was no way she'd eat the synthetic stuff after what happened to Mama.

In the morning, I dragged myself from bed and got

ready for school without much thought. I couldn't think about anything but Mama. Alone. In the basement. And how it would be when the FBVA showed up at our door.

My stomach twisted in knots as I went over it and over it. It twisted so bad I could barely feel the butterflies until they fluttered to my heart, speeding it up so I got all hot and cold with sweat.

My entire world had just broken into teeny-tiny pieces of "oh no" that made me want to cry and run and hide.

And it looked like the Duke felt the same way.

She sat at the dining room table, pale with the same dark circles under her eyes. Her hair still braided, but all fuzzy from sleeping on them. In front of where I usually sat was a banana, and I couldn't help when the tears came.

I stood there, in a too-quiet house filled with the scent of garlic and air freshener—instead of burned bacon, pan-scraped eggs, and the familiar off-tune lilt of Mama's bad singing.

The Duke was on me before the first tear even reached my cheek.

"Sit down, kiddo." Placing a firm hand around

my shoulder, she guided me to the table. "It's all right. Everything will be all right."

But it couldn't be all right. "I know."

I sat, and she knelt next to me.

"When I was a girl," she began softly, placing a cold hand over mine, "my father was a boat builder. We lived in a small fishing village, but his boats were sought after throughout the jarldoms. The gods had blessed his hands with skill and his head with vision. One day a woman came to our village. She wanted a fleet of ships built to sail across the known ocean to search for a mythical island, richer than we could imagine. Filled with the gold of a new faith. Of Christianity. My father could not promise this woman a fleet. He had several men to help, but she wanted ten ships built in two months."

I wanted to ask what any of this had to do with Mama or the FBVA but bit down on the inside of my cheek to keep from asking. She had this faraway look on her face, and her voice was . . . sad.

"He told her it would be impossible," she continued. "But the woman smiled and said if he did this for her, she would pay a fortune, find men to help him finish, and give his daughter, me, a place on one of her ships. I was your age, Sophie. Headstrong but generally obedient. A good daughter. A good sister. Still, I didn't want to go train to be a shield-maiden, even though it was an honor and would bring prestige to my family. To not just be a Norseman, but to become a Viking. That was no life for someone like me—raiding, stealing, killing. I didn't want riches or fame. I wanted a simple life. But my father had different plans."

"He made you go?" I asked.

She nodded, a small smile tugging her lips. "He did. And I became a warrior, while he enjoyed his newfound riches. I was taken from my family, Sophie. From my mother. My sisters. My brothers. I was taken, and thrown into a ship where my only possessions were hidden in a small sack and shoved under the bench I shared with three other rowers." Her tone deepened, getting raspy. Jaw clenched, she searched my face before getting to the point. "And I survived. My world didn't exist anymore, but I adapted. My blood may not run through your veins, but you are my daughter. You have my strength. My power. My love. And I will *never* throw you in a boat, Sophie... or let them take you from me. Do you understand?"

I nodded. I did understand. Perfectly. And I loved her for that with all my heart. I was thrown onto a boat once, but the Duke and Mama had saved me.

"Good." She stood in a hurry and placed her hands on her hips. "Things are weird right now, and I don't know how to use the stove, so . . . banana for breakfast, okay?"

I nodded again, afraid to say anything in case I started sobbing.

"I'm calling the school to tell them you're sick."

My eyes widened as a jolt of panic lit my heart on fire. "But if I don't go to school, they'll think something is wrong, and then CPS might show up and find Mama in the basement, and they'll call the FBVA and—"

"Enough." She cut me off, but not in the I'm-in-trouble voice. She sounded . . . surprised. "If I call to say you're sick, they'll think you're sick. If you go to school today, they'll know something's wrong. You're as pale as me, and about as ragged."

"But . . ." I didn't know what I wanted to say, or what to even argue. I sure didn't want to go to school, but I didn't want to stay home alone with Mama in the basement either.

"No buts, kiddo. You and me are taking the day off."

Oh. "You're going to work from home?" I knew I sounded more excited than I should have, but relief made my voice a bit squeaky.

"No. No work. If we're to come out of this together, Sophie, we're going to have to take a little trip."

We were. "Where are we going?"

"I've asked for an audience with the Council at their meeting today in Philly. They told me to show up at noon and they'd try to hear us."

"Will they help?" The Duke never said nice things about the Council and tried to stay far away from them. The Council made sure all vampires followed the vampire code, and judged complaints and things. But the Duke said they didn't like vampires that voted to walk into the light, and most of the Council was against it.

I watched as she pressed her lips together, and a whole minute passed before she relaxed them. "They're going to listen to what I have to say, and I need you there to help me."

Something deep down sparked with pride as she said that. But I wasn't sure how I could help. "What do you need me to do?"

"Eat your breakfast." Bending, she kissed the top of my head as I eyed the banana. "That's all I need you to do."

"Mom?" I asked.

"Hmm?"

"Can ... before we go ..." I trailed off as I turned the banana in my hands. "Can I ... see her?"

If the Duke were human, this would be where she'd hold her breath or tear up. If she were human, and hadn't lived a thousand years and been to war when she was my age, she'd say absolutely not.

But the Duke wasn't human. She was superhuman. And my mom.

"Do you promise to eat that banana?" she asked.

I turned in my chair and nodded when my eyes met hers.

"Good. Then yes. I'll take you to see her. I'll need to change after and gather my thoughts if I'm to lay out my plan to the Council."

She had a plan? Plans were good. Really good.

Because Delphine was going to try and contact Anon715 today, and the more plans we had, the better.

Chapter 11

Sitting in the Mercedes, barely noticing the world whizzing by, I wished I hadn't gone into the basement. I'd turned around and left almost as soon as I'd walked in.

Mama, sitting there, all tied up to a pillar, her eyes full red with dried blood in her hair and on her skin, I...I couldn't stay there. I could still hear her screech, like metal scratching down glass, but louder. And weirder. And it froze my insides solid.

"You all right?" asked the Duke.

"Yeah, Mom." We'd been driving for about forty-five minutes. I only knew because I'd checked the time when we left, because it was . . . normal. So was pulling the seat belt, clicking it in place, turning on the radio, changing the channel.

Normal. Regular. Ordinary.

"You're a bad liar, Sophie."

I smiled a little and glanced at her. She'd changed into another power suit, complete with six-inch heels, and had fixed her battle braids in the time it took me to force down the banana bite by bite.

She looked fierce. Ready for action. And I was glad.

"Look, when we get there, there are a few things you need to know."

That didn't sound good. "Oh?"

"They don't normally allow humans into the chamber, so when we go in, you need to hold on to my hand. Tight. Got it?"

I nodded, but her eyes were on the road so I backed it with a quick, "Yes, Mom."

"Good. Next, you keep your eyes on the floor. Don't look at the Council unless they speak to you. Though I doubt they will. But just in case."

My heart skipped a little as dread spread thick

and heavy in my belly. "What if they *do* speak to me?"

She was quiet for a minute, concentrating on the highway sign up ahead. Then the blinker started ticking and she pulled into the exit lane. "Nothing. Don't say a word. You can look at them, but that's it. It's like a ... trick."

I must've made a weird face, because she looked at me as she swerved for the exit.

"Do you remember what I told you about vampires, Sophie?" she asked, her voice more than a little serious.

Lots. She'd told me so much I didn't know what she wanted me to say. That most meant well and wanted normal human-like lives. But that some hated that vampires had voted to walk in the light and wished it never happened. Some were cruel. Evil. But most were kind. Really, really trying to fit in.

There was a code vampires had followed for close to a thousand years. "Is this about the code thing?"

The Duke snorted. "The code thing. Yes. When we walked into the light, the Council split up. There were twelve, but each one chose a key country to live in so they could form mini Councils with local representatives. It makes it easier. Before, if we had a problem, we'd have to lie and glamour our way onto an airplane to France."

Glamour. I shuddered. At least that was illegal now.

"We're lucky the US chapter is here, in Philly. It's the original capital of the United States, you know." The Duke pursed her lips as she merged into traffic. "The members of the Council are old."

"As old as you?" I asked.

"Older."

That one word took away my breath. The Duke was the oldest vampire in Hopetown. "How much older?"

She chuckled. "A *lot* older. Ancient. They've survived this long because they're the most power-ful vampires in the world. The code is everything to them, and if you break it, that's it. I shouldn't even be bringing you. I'm just hoping that seeing us here, together, will remind Lord Aaheru—the leader of the Council—of the importance of family, and strengthen our case. When I say you do not speak even when spoken to, you do not speak even when spoken to. Got it?"

"It's against the code?" My voice sounded small, but I was still stuck on how old the Council was.

"A human may not speak in their presence."

Then I'd keep my lips glued shut and hope I wouldn't be tested.

I was surprised when we arrived.

We pulled into a hotel parking garage and walked a few blocks into the heart of Old City Philadelphia, its old-timey redbrick buildings feeling out of place against the backdrop of metal skyscrapers shooting into the sky. Trees lined the streets, and signs tacked on redbrick walls told tourists this and that about something to do with the War of Independence.

I remembered being here for a field trip a few years back, and I supposed if an ancient vampire council had made Philly its headquarters, Old City was the most likely spot.

But I wasn't prepared for the inside because the building looked historic from the outside. We walked through the modern reception area and followed signs for the "chamber." Everything was bright electric light, with black-and-white canvas photos of the Philadelphia skyline hung on the light green walls. I followed the Duke as she wound through the hallways, until we came to a set of open double doors. There were rows of chairs inside, where a few vamps sat, waiting their turn. And at the back, on a raised stage, there was a long table with twelve nicely dressed vampires sitting—looking very official.

"Next on the docket, the young vampire Selene versus the Elder vampire Godfric."

The clickety-clack of one of those courtroom typewriters pinged as another vampire took notes.

As the Duke squeezed my hand and we stepped into the chamber, I did what she'd told me to do and glued my eyes to the tiled floor.

"I call a halt!" The Duke's voice boomed, and I heard the shuffle of vampires turning in their seats, and cringed at the silence that followed.

"Who dares call a halt to these proceedings?" A woman's voice. Pleasant, but kind of annoyed.

"Freyja Knutsdatter."

A hum of interest went through the chamber, and the Duke gave my hand another squeeze as she led us down the aisle.

I watched her heels—one in front of the other, heel-toe, heel-toe. So confident. She made it look so easy. I didn't think I'd ever be able to walk in heels, especially not like that.

"The halt is granted." Another voice, this time a guy.

"Explain yourself, Freyja." Back to the woman. "You dare call a halt, and bring a human before the Council? When you contacted this Council, we were very clear that we would hear your concerns *if* there was time."

"I will explain myself to Lord Aaheru, and to him alone."

Another murmur went through the chamber, raising the little hairs on my arms.

"Order!" The guy again. He waited for everyone to quiet down before continuing. "Freyja Knutsdatter. Lord Aaheru no longer presides over public Council and refuses to meet with anyone."

"He'll meet with me. Bring me to him." This

time, as the Duke used her boardroom voice, the crowd was louder. Outrage mixed with shock, and that scared me. But she told me I'd be safe, that she'd keep me safe, so I stepped even closer to her.

"Order!"

A chair scraped against the floor, and the sound of footsteps was almost swallowed by the restless crowd.

"She can't ask this—" the woman began, but the gentleman cut her off.

"She can, and did," he said.

"But—"

"Silence." I was pretty sure all sound got sucked out of the room as the guy's voice boomed. "Freyja Knutsdatter is an Elder. She has the right. This way."

The Duke gave my hand another squeeze and led the way again. We veered right, and I could see the edge of the stage out of the corner of my eye.

"This was bold, Freyja." The man was directly in front of us—I could see the tips of his polished leather shoes. We stopped.

"Desperate times, desperate measures, Thomas."

He sighed, one of those really long ones, before

speaking again. "You should leave her out here. The lord will do his best to trip her up."

"No. She has to come with me."

"She'll be safe—"

"It isn't that, Thomas. I come on a...family matter."

"Ah." There was something about that "ah" I didn't like.

"Sophie might remind him of his own family."

Silence. Then I watched as the tips of his shoes disappeared, and we were moving again.

Chapter 12

We passed through another bright, pale green hallway to a staircase. And when we got to the top, we were shown into a big, dark room. The curtains were pulled shut, with lit candles as the only light. I took a deep breath, and the smell of fresh cotton dryer sheets mixed with patchouli incense almost made me sneeze.

I couldn't tell much else about the room, because my eyes were still glued to the floor, but there was carpet. Maybe when my eyes adjusted I'd be able to tell what color it was. But right now I was busy trying not to sneeze while being weirdly aware of a change in atmosphere. Like when Mama turned on the really old TV she kept in the living room.

Mama's TV was big and bulky with an antenna on top, and knobs and dials on a panel next to the curved screen.

When that old hunk of junk turned on, it made a whiny noise, and a blast of electricity changed something in the air that made every little hair on my body stand on end.

The same thing happened when we stepped into the room, but with it came an awful sinking feeling. I squeezed the Duke's hand. She squeezed back.

"Freyja Knutsdatter," said the man, Thomas, who'd led the way.

"Hmm. Leave us." The new voice, another guy, was like melted candle wax—warm and smooth.

I heard Thomas leave, closing the door behind him. And then there was nothing.

Silence.

Not even from the Duke.

The *thud-ump* of my heartbeat echoed in my ears, and I almost forgot to breathe.

"Freyja Knutsdatter," the new voice finally said.

"Oh, Benevolent Lord." The Duke tugged my hand as she sank to her knees, and I hurried to copy her. If the Duke was groveling, this vampire must be the real deal. If I wasn't scared before—which I had been—I sure was now. "Aaheru the Great, Pharaoh of Pharaohs, Protector of Your Children."

"Up, up." The voice sounded almost bored, but the Duke made no move to stand. Maybe it was one of those tricks she'd told me about, a rule he wanted her to break. "I was surprised when I got word of your request to speak to the Council. Must be... serious. And you have brought an offering?"

An...? Oh God. That must be me. The second I realized it, sweat broke out across my forehead, and I was sure his vampire super-ears heard my heart skitter to a stop.

"Not an offering, Your Benevolence. This is my daughter. We come before you today concerning a family matter."

A scratch and hiss. A match. And the glow of a large candle brightened the room a bit. It was scented, and now a blast of lemon zest mixed with the fresh cotton patchouli mash-up, and my stomach churned.

Breathing through my mouth, I tried to focus.

"Let me look at you, child."

Yikes. For a second, I thought he was talking to me, but as I took a deep breath—and tried not to vomit—the Duke rose to her feet, her hand slipping from mine, but I stayed where I was. My 1,200-year-old mom. A...child? I knew she'd said he was an Ancient, but how much older than her could he be?

"Ah, Freyja. You haven't changed. It's been a long time, hasn't it? The French Revolution, I think?"

"As memorable as that was, Your Benevolence, the last time we met was during the Great Famine."

"Ireland, then. Time is...muddy. I suppose the famine *was* more recent." He chuckled softly, but the Duke didn't answer. I didn't blame her but didn't think much about it, because...nausea. "I have missed you, shield-maiden. And now you have discarded your calling as one of my elite guards to don the mantle of mother, to this...human. Stand, human."

Rude. Well, not really. But the way he said it made it sound like an insult, and as I did what he asked, I didn't know whether to be scared or angry.

Until the Duke found my hand, and I was safe again. My mom was here. And this guy would help us.

"What is your name, little one?"

I automatically opened my mouth but quickly shut it. Wow. Rule number one, no talking. And I almost blew it. I blamed the weird mix of smells. How was I supposed to concentrate?

He laughed, and with a gentle whoosh of air, a pair of bare feet appeared right in front of my sneakers. Blinking rapidly, I fought the urge to cry out and focused. There were rings on his toes, but I barely had time to count how many—seven, all golden—before the vampire tipped my chin so I had to look up at him.

Crap. My eyes widened with the sudden movement, and my pulse jerked to high-speed. I didn't know what I was expecting, but when I saw him for the first time, my brows knotted together. He was...young. Like maybe twentysomething. And he was supposed to be ancient? Sometimes the vampire thing was so confusing.

He wore a cream, cable-knit sweater over straight-legged jeans. Really normal. Except for the black-and-gold makeup he wore, like something out of a mummy movie.

"To be a parent is to be a god," he said to the Duke. "A family matter, you said?"

"Yes, Your Benevolence."

"Involving the FBVA?" He spat the question as if it tasted like week-old gym socks.

"Yes, Your Benevolence."

He sighed and took a step back. "This was not anticipated, this... whatever is making us go rogue. Dr. Bennington was supposed to be our savior. Our advocate."

"Indeed, Your Benevolence. But Dr. Bennington has made almost no strides since his appointment to the FBVA. He's failing us."

Free to look at him, since he spoke to me, I watched as a muscle below his cheek twitched. "Still, Dr. Bennington is one of our only allies in the White House, Freyja Knutsdatter. He has the ear of the president, and the lives of so many depend upon that. I have no power in this arena. Both our North American Councils are monitored closely for signs of dissent. Whatever it is you seek, I won't be able to assist."

"But it's *Marie*." I jumped a little at the Duke's outburst, and the Aaheru dude whipped his head around to glare at her. "You came when I called you to France, to save her from the queen's fate. And again in Ireland when the famine killed a million where they stood, and we starved along with them. You helped us. *Saved* us. All I ask is for a small contingent. Enough vampires to fend them off while I figure out a way to move her. It might ease with time, and I have her contained. No one was hurt, and the FBVA wasn't alerted."

Aaheru's face softened a little, but he shook his head. "Yet. The FBVA hasn't been alerted *yet*. This is beyond my control, Freyja. How did you think this would go? That I'd send a small army into a human neighborhood? You think your neighbors would be comfortable with that? That they wouldn't call the authorities, and the FBVA wouldn't show up asking questions? To do this would start a war. It would jeopardize the delicate relationship we have with the human president. *You* voted to walk into the light—against my counsel—and now we must all play by their rules. You did this."

I glanced at the Duke, kind of surprised that my diplomatic parent might have thought about starting a war, and even more surprised that everything Aaheru said made complete sense to me. But when I saw bloody tears pooling in her lower lids, despite the angry set of her jaw, I felt my own tears come.

"You turned Marie from human to vampire, and that makes her your *daughter*. I'm just asking for ... time."

My eyes widened. Did that make Aaheru my grandfather? Or was it different with vampires?

"Time for what, Freyja, shield-maiden of Thor? Have you evidence of trickery? Are any of the rumors true? My team tells me there are discussions online suggesting there might be a cure."

"Of course I have no evidence. But Marie went rogue after feasting on a new form of synthetic blood, and I don't believe in coincidences."

As I looked at her, she drew herself up to full height and squared her shoulders.

Aaheru nodded and pursed his lips, then glanced from the Duke to me, and back again. "I am sorry," he said, clasping his hands behind his back as he walked toward a bookshelf. "Marie was always one of my favorites, but I cannot jeopardize our relationship with Dr. Bennington."

The Duke said nothing but watched him like a hawk as I turned my head. Marie. The way he could say Mama's name after telling us he'd do nothing to help her. Us.

"Unless you can uncover evidence of the FBVA's true intent, or the existence of a cure. If you can do that, I will send a contingent to assist and ensure the Council deals with Dr. Bennington."

"We don't have time for that. Not without you." The words ground through the Duke's teeth. "I need help keeping her calm."

"Well, then might we end our discussion with a little advice? Don't fear your time in the camp, Freyja. Their goal is to rehabilitate."

"So they say." This time, a little bite broke through the Duke's careful calm.

"Ah," he said, a bright sound, like he found something funny. I looked at him. He pulled a book from the shelf, opened it, and removed an envelope. "And now we get to the crux of the matter. You don't trust the rehabilitation facility, Freyja Knutsdatter. You don't trust the very humans you longed to live with. Well."

He turned, a smirk creasing his makeup as he made his way back to us.

"I see you, Freyja. I see straight through you, and

down into the spark that still remains. I see the shield-maiden, rejected by your birth father, terrified and alone in a Norwegian forest. Turned into a vampire by a villain, a sire who thought to leave you so you could ravage your own people when hunger overcame you and there was no choice but to slaughter them. I saw it then, when I found you, took you, nurtured you, taught you. And I see it still."

The Duke's eyes narrowed as Aaheru looked at me, his smirk turning into a smile. A toothy, fangy smile.

"But this little one." Aaheru stepped closer and cupped my cheeks. "She did not ask for what's about to happen. Innocent. Ignorant of the wanton, willful destruction of our shadow empire."

As quickly as he took my face in his hands, he let go, and turned his attention to the Duke. She was taller than him, and he looked so weak next to her. So lean. So . . . not powerful.

"I've been fond of you, Freyja. And Marie. My truest child. The one who never rebelled or thought to usurp me."

"But none of that matters because you won't help in our greatest time of need."

He fell silent and glanced at me. I shivered.

"They are always your greatest time of need, are they not? This will be surpassed by another." He jerked his head in my direction, and the Duke pursed her lips. "I may not be able to help you without clear evidence of a gross overstep, but I could see your daughter safe."

"Thank you, Your Benevolence." But the Duke's words were short and clipped.

"There is a place. You'll find the details in here." Aaheru handed the envelope to the Duke, who hesitated a little, her fingers shaking. If he noticed, he didn't show it. Instead, Aaheru waved his hand and took one last look at me. "No thanks for this lifesaving boon, little one?"

But I knew the drill. He wouldn't trick me into talking.

And he'd upset my mom.

Instead, I nodded and bowed, like I'd seen people do in Mama's black-and-white movies.

I wasn't one hundred percent sure what just happened, but if the Duke had expected help for Mama from Aaheru, it was going to be a *long* drive home.

Chapter 13

I hated being right. The drive back to Hopetown was long and silent.

Aaheru's envelope sat in the center console, unopened, and I wasn't sure what to think. Maybe I should've asked why she didn't push more, but the way she gripped the steering wheel made me nope that idea.

She needed a stress ball.

"That was...interesting," I said, breaking the half-hour-long silence.

When she didn't answer, I sighed. Of course she didn't, and I had zero idea how to help, but we couldn't keep this up. The car had always been our safe place.

I wanted to talk, to word-vomit all my fears and feelings. And cry. I wanted to cry so bad, to let it all out and not stop until all this was over.

I needed my mom. My Duke.

I didn't see her take a hand off the wheel, but as she put it over mine, it was like someone let air out of a balloon. Everything shifted, and I grabbed on with my other hand.

"Do you want music?" Defeated. That's how she sounded.

"No, thanks."

She nodded, and an easier question popped into my head. Something kind of neutral, kind of not.

"Who's Dr. Bennington?" I asked.

Giving my hand a squeeze, the Duke smiled. "Just a doctor. A vampire. He was made head of the FBVA and reports directly to the president. Which is why Aaheru needs proof of something bad happening before he can step in. He's right. Bennington is our link to the White House. He can't be seen sending vampires to help us. It could cause tensions between the FBVA and the vampire community."

The head of the FBVA was a vampire? My brows shot up.

"Something's not right with all this," she said.

"Definitely."

She sighed and half turned to look at me. "I'm going to drop you at Delphine's, all right? School's out, so no one will take notice if you go over there."

Good. I needed to talk to Delphine. "Where are *you* going?"

"I need to check on Mama, and think about next steps."

Next steps. A plan.

Like figuring out what to do, and how me and Delphine would make it happen.

"You were *where*?" Delphine's jaw dropped so low I thought it would dislocate. We sat in her bedroom, surrounded by posters of K-pop stars and her huge bobblehead doll collection. She told me that each year she picked something to focus on or learn about, to help keep boredom away. I supposed when you were twelve forever, it would get boring pretty fast. Three years ago, she collected every bobblehead she could find. Two years ago, she studied astronomy. Last year, she learned everything she could about sharks. And this year was all about K-pop and learning how to mix music. Her old playlists were filled with classical music and bad, creepy recordings of lost tracks from the twenties. But not anymore.

Behind the posters, DIY decal ponies ran and frolicked (they were old and peeling, but her mom did her best given they were adopting a twelve-year-old . . . eight years ago) against lavender-painted walls. It was everything a sophisticated, three-hundred-year-old vampire never knew they wanted.

"Aaheru?" she asked . . . for the second time. "You met *Aaheru?"*

Third time. Her voice climbed with every syllable, and I winced.

"Yeah. He's a weird dude."

"Weird?" Apparently I said the wrong thing,

because Delphine's eyes almost crossed as she shrieked. "He is an *Ancient*, Sophie Dawes. Revered and . . . and . . ."

"Old?" I asked.

"Respected." She gave me one of those *really?* looks, but I shrugged. Aaheru's awesomeness wasn't what I wanted to talk about. Neither was the mountain of homework she'd handed me. Okay, maybe not a mountain, but also very low on my list of priorities.

"What was he like?" Delphine scooted closer on the bed, and I pursed my lips.

"He looked really young but acted really serious. He even called the Duke 'child.' "

"Young like me, or . . . ?"

"No, an adult. Like twentysomething."

A shadow crossed Delphine's pale face, and she stood abruptly. "Wow. I'm impressed." But she didn't sound impressed. She sounded annoyed. "I've never met an Ancient. That could be nice, calling twelve-hundred-year-old vamps 'child' from a throne while sipping from my pony thermos. At least you'll get to grow up and be treated like an adult. Me? It doesn't matter how old I am in vampire years. All humans and vampires see is a kid."

I shifted on the bed and focused on the pony-patterned comforter. I didn't need to look to know Delphine's shoulders were slumped, or that she was probably chewing on her right pinky nail. The age she turned, and the problems it caused, didn't really come up often.

"I . . . I didn't mean to upset you."

"Pish posh," she exclaimed, switching from sad to fake happy in a second. "It's all right. You're so very lucky, you know? I was alone for hundreds of years before my parents adopted me. But you, you have your whole life ahead of you, and you not only have your moms to guide you, but your *birth* mother too. That's really amazing."

I smiled. "I mean, fair. But only if I write back to her."

"Well, you *should*," Delphine said softly, her lips tugging into a frown. "Human life is short, Sophie. Don't waste precious time when you could have your other mom in your life."

I pressed my lips together as a flush heated my cheeks. Tara Washington *wasn't* my "other mom." She was the woman who gave birth to me. I didn't know her, and I definitely didn't want to listen to whatever excuses she had for giving me away.

"But I don't need her in my life. I *have* parents," I retorted.

"What I mean is—" Delphine cleared her throat. "They know you love them. And it might not be a bad idea to make contact. In case."

"In case what?" My heart fluttered in my chest. I knew the answer: in case the Duke and Mama couldn't be my family anymore. In case I didn't end up in the facility and needed a new mom. I shook my head. "Never mind. We have more important things to think about."

"I know." Delphine sighed. "Just...think about it."

It was time for a major subject change. "So? Did you message Anon715?"

"Yes, but no response yet."

"Girls?" A knock sounded right after the call, and Delphine walked to the door. It was Delphine's mom, wearing a bright green tee that looked amazing against her tanned skin. But it clashed with her orange bracelet and denim shorts. "I thought you two might want some snacks. Cookies for Sophie and warmed blood for you, sweetie. You two doing okay in here?"

Mrs. Abernathy's smile was brighter than the "diamond" necklace I'd bought Mama for Mother's Day last year. I'd saved up all my chore money and gone to the Allentown Mall with the Duke to one of those department stores to spend every last cent. And Mama had cried when she'd opened it. Red hot tears of blood for that tiny pendant.

And as I nodded at Mrs. Abernathy, who didn't know what to do or say, the sting of I miss-my-mama tears made me squeeze my eyes shut while Delphine took the snacks.

"Thanks, Mom. We're just peachy, though Sophie here doesn't have much mind for homework."

"Of course you don't, Sophie." She sighed. "You know we're here for you, right? We've always been there for your family like you've always been there for us. Anything you need, you just ask."

But when I didn't answer, she cleared her throat.

"I'll leave you girls to it. Do whatever homework you can. Dinner's at six."

Delphine waved as her mom backed out of the room, but when the door closed, she straightened her spine.

"We need to get on the interweb and find out more about this Dr. Bennington."

I blinked a few times to clear up the tears, and to give me a minute to figure out what she was talking about. "Internet. Right."

With a sigh, I got up and went straight to her computer desk.

"You never mentioned Bennington before," I said, pulling up a browser as she grabbed a spare folding chair from the closet. Delphine knew how to work the internet—she had to, for homework—but she preferred to have me do all the searching for her when I was over, because anything modern made her uncomfortable.

"Just another politician, and very rarely in the news." She wrinkled her nose at the screen and sat next to me. "Until you mentioned him, I'd forgotten he existed, never mind that he's a vampire."

So much for keeping vamps happy, if vamps barely knew about Bennington.

"That's a lot of Benningtons," she said, leaning forward as the search engine did its thing. The first page? A local dermatologist.

"Lemme just..." I deleted my search for Dr. Bennington and typed: "Dr. Bennington FBVA."

That was better. I clicked the first link, and we both started reading.

A lot of background, schools he went to, but no photos or video clips. Except one. A single head-shot on the FBVA website. Thin with close-cropped brown hair. Bennington looked like any other guy.

"I don't recognize him, but he must be old-school," Delphine murmured. Right, because vampires used to avoid being in paintings or photos—in case anyone figured out they lived forever. Made sense. "He was probably required to have a photo for the website."

But then Delphine and I sat up straight. Bennington's lead research facility for the United States was moved about a year ago from California to the FBVA facility right here, just outside Hopetown.

I arched my brows. That was an odd coincidence. Especially since there were almost no cases of rogue vampires in the Northeast until recently. Most were on the West Coast. And hadn't Lisa at the blood bank said the FBVA had been trying to get the donor policy changed for over a year?

Delphine grabbed my arm and pointed to the screen. "Sophie, look."

Yada yada, official government position. Blah blah, studying rogue vampires, working on a cure—

My eyes widened, and a shiver ran up my spine. Bennington wasn't only the head of the FBVA, he was the founder of SynCorps. The blood bank.

The same blood bank that made a deal with the state of Pennsylvania to stop paying donors for blood and force vamps to buy the synthetic stuff that turned Mama rogue.

And it looked like SynCorps had bought a ton of small, local, and noncorporate blood banks last year and now controlled *all* the blood banks in the country.

"Seek and ye shall find," Delphine said, drawing out the words. "Looks like our Dr. Bennington has some explaining to do. And here, look. Bennington was part of the original research team that discovered how to make synthetic blood!"

Holy moly. Her desktop notification went off with a *ping*, and my eyes followed the pop-up message at the bottom of the screen.

"Delphine?"

"Yeah?"

I pointed at the message and grinned. "Looks like Anon715 just got back to you."

She smiled and clicked on the message. "Are you thinking what I'm thinking, Sophie Dawes?"

I wasn't sure what she was thinking. But if Anon715 had the proof they claimed to have, and if that proof was that Bennington was behind turning vampires rogue . . .

Then that meant Aaheru would have to help us.

Chapter 14

Okay. Things didn't exactly go as planned with Anon715. They wouldn't send us any proof over the internet because they had no idea if we were telling the truth about who we were. For all they knew, we were undercover police. But it turned out they lived in Hopetown and were willing to meet us at Chuck's Chocolate House after school. That way we would feel safe being somewhere familiar, and there'd be people around. Their message did read like a kid—filled with emojis and letters for words—but that wasn't a guarantee. These were internet rules one and two—never talk to strangers online...and don't meet them in real life.

Delphine did point out that even if she was twelve, she still had vampire strength and could keep us safe. But I still needed to think about it. Without something to prove they had evidence that could convince Aaheru to help, I wasn't willing to meet them.

When I got home, I fell into my bed but barely slept. Mama had been banging the pipes all night. And the next morning, I was so tired, I just couldn't believe my ears when the Duke told me her plan.

"I'm not doing it," I said, my eyes wide as I stared at the Duke across the dining room table. In the distance, a half-hearted clang echoed, and I turned to glance at the basement door across the hall.

The Duke didn't look up from her newspaper or flinch at the noise. Instead, she held up a banana and set it down on my place setting.

"You don't refuse an Ancient, Sophie. Lord Aaheru's safe house is the best place to be right now."

"It's in Arizona!"

"It is." How did she do that? How did she stay so calm?

Scowling, I sat at the table and folded my arms over my chest. "And what are you going to do?"

"Stay here with Mama." *Bang.*

Hot tears pricked my eyes and I nodded. If she sent me to live with strangers—for my own good—then someone had to stay and protect Mama. I knew that. I got it. But there was something so chilly about how calm she was. Like it was easy to send me across the country. Alone. With no one who cared about me. Or loved me. And the name "Tara Washington" flashed through my mind.

It was easy for her too. Abandoning me. Did Tara Washington even care when she handed me over to the adoption agency? Did she even think about what she was doing, and how it would affect me?

I could never do that to someone I loved.

But here was the Duke, my mom, who'd given me a home and no reason to feel unsafe, calmly talking about doing the same thing Tara Washington had done twelve years ago.

Abandoning me. *Bang.*

"I don't want to go." My voice was a little croaky, thick with discomfort. "I want to stay here, with you."

"You can't." With a sigh, the Duke slowly folded her paper in half, then in half again, before placing it on the table. She wouldn't look at me, and I really wished she would. "Listen. Delphine's parents won't be able to donate blood again. Delphine's going to need it if we can't get organic blood anymore. It's only a matter of time before I'm going to have to drink that synthetic stuff. Then if you're right and there's something in it, it's game over. How are you going to contain me, kiddo? You're not. And I can't figure out how to get whatever evidence Aaheru needs to step in. Then there's this."

Reaching into her pocket, she pulled out a slip of paper and slid it across the table. But I didn't care. I hadn't even thought about the blood situation and how the Duke was going to eat. I bit down on my lower lip to keep the sob in my throat from rising. I was too tired for this. Too . . . done.

"Sophie."

I looked at her and realized she was staring right at me. Like I wanted. But her eyes were bloodshot, and there were telltale smudges of blood on her lower lids. She'd been crying, like I wanted to cry.

Numb, I reached over and snatched the paper

from the table as my stomach flipped. This was too much. Everything was way too much.

The Duke nodded, then sat back and folded her arms across her chest.

I turned the paper over, and a wave of ice crashed into me. I couldn't breathe.

> Stopped by after receiving a call from the neighborhood watch. Will call again tomorrow. Laura.

CPS was here while we were in Philly, and someone *had* heard the commotion the night before. My tummy knotted up. *Bang.*

"I must have just missed her when I got home yesterday. We're running out of time on both fronts." The Duke spat the words, and I lifted heavy, tear-lined eyes to meet hers. My chest felt like it was caving in, crushing my heart and lungs, making it hard to breathe. "CPS will come. The FBVA will come. And they *will* take Mama, and anyone else who's here. The only thing I can do is get you away. See you safe, because I'm not going down without a fight. Do you understand?"

"Y-yes." I was wrong. The Duke wasn't abandoning me. She was going to war. A one vampire standoff. But I could help. I could—

Ding-dong.

A jolt of fear zipped through my body, forcing a thin layer of sweat through my skin. My eyes widened. It was maybe 6:30 a.m.

"Mom—" I began, but she held up a hand as she sniffed the air.

"Go upstairs and get dressed," she said.

"Is that them? Aaheru's people? Are they here to take me away?" Because why else would someone be at the door so early?

"No. Delphine's parents volunteered to drive you to Arizona, but they can't just drop everything to do it. It'll be a day or two. Hopefully just a day." She rose, hands planted on the table as the doorbell rang again. "Hurry. Run upstairs and get dressed. I'll let her in."

"Who?"

The Duke sniffed the air one last time, then turned to me, fire in her bloody eyes.

"It's Laura. CPS is here."

Chapter 15

I was pretty sure we were in serious trouble. How were we going to make sure Mama kept quiet? If Laura heard her . . .

I didn't remember going upstairs, finding clothes, getting dressed, or going back downstairs. How was any of this even happening?

When I walked into the living room, it was like everything was in slow motion, even conversation, so that Laura and the Duke sounded like aliens, all deep voiced and not making sense.

But they were both looking at me. And their mouths were moving.

Against the pink carpet, pink curtains, and pink furniture it reminded me of something out of one of those horror movies the Duke liked to watch. The ones with all the blood.

I shook my head and tried to focus on the non-pink things in the room. The bookcase. The fireplace. The really old, really big TV sitting on a wooden stand in the corner complete with some sort of video player thing. A VRC? RVC? I could never remember the right letters.

"Sophie?" Laura's face was scrunched up with concern, and I did my best to smile.

"Hi."

"Hi, sweetie." She took a step forward. "Your mom told me what happened."

No way. My eyes widened. I looked at the Duke, but before I could say anything, she crossed the room to stand next to me and placed a hand on my shoulder.

"It's been rough on her. On us," she said, all quiet and calm. "Marie will come home soon. She just needs some space."

I blinked rapidly, trying to figure out what lie the Duke had just told Laura.

"I can imagine." Laura looked right at me. "I'm sorry, Sophie. Grown-ups... well, grown-ups sometimes need a little time apart. I'm sure things will work out." What...? She turned to the Duke. "Maybe you and I should discuss this in private. I can set up some counseling sessions for Sophie."

"Counseling?" I echoed, furrowing my brow.

"It's okay, kiddo." The Duke pulled me into a hug. "Everything will be all right. Mama will be home soon." Then quick as lightning, the Duke bent her head and whispered in my ear. "Mama and I got into an argument, and she left to stay with friends for a few days, okay?"

Um. I mean, Mama sometimes got angry about things, but to say she left, even for a while, was a pretty serious stretch.

"I know you're on your way to school. I just wanted to check in. I was worried when we got the call about a disturbance the other night. And when no one was home yesterday afternoon, well. I'm sorry for the intrusion."

I looked at Laura. She seemed genuinely sad, and

I felt awful. On the one hand, it was Laura's job to make sure I was safe. But on the other hand, if we didn't lie, we'd all end up in the facility. If the choice was Mama, or Laura...I would absolutely choose Mama.

"I can come to the office today at lunchtime to make a statement," said the Duke. "I'm sure she'll be home in a day or two. I never should have said anything about the food."

"The food?" Laura asked.

"I thought it was time for Sophie to start learning how to cook, because...well." The Duke shrugged and smiled a little. Totally convincing. "Has my wife ever cooked for you, Laura?"

Laura nodded but glanced at me as she pursed her lips. There was fear in her eyes, like she wanted me to tell her things weren't all right, and that she needed to save me. But I stared back, blank, and when she spoke, her voice sounded all forced. "I'm so sorry. That must have been a tough conversation."

I don't know. Maybe it was the way she looked at me, but anger bubbled in my chest. I remembered all the times Mama proudly served Laura her food, trying to be perfect. To fit in. And Laura knew that. It was why Laura always said "thank you" and took a bite or two.

I thought Laura was being nice. But now I wondered if she'd always just been waiting for something to go wrong, if she believed everything in the movies and TV about vampires was true.

Vampires were dangerous.

Vampires could go rogue at any minute.

Vampires couldn't be trusted.

It was one thing at school, where the kids and teachers had always been a little scared of me because of my parents. But Laura was different. Laura was part of my life—even if it was an annoying part of my life—and I felt so betrayed.

"We need to get moving," I said, needing to get out of the room before I screamed. "We'll be late."

Bang. Bang. Bang.

The Duke stiffened as Laura frowned and glanced around.

"Pipes," the Duke explained, smiling a little. "We just had a new central air conditioner installed.

I need to call the HVAC guys again. I think they missed a connection."

Laura pursed her lips as her eyes slid to Mama's doll shelves. Empty.

"What happened to Marie's collection?"

Crap. I pressed my lips together. Tight. And Laura chose that exact moment to whip around and look at me.

"She took them," the Duke said, smooth as creamy peanut butter.

Bang. That one was way louder, and Laura dropped her pen as we all jumped. It rolled under Mama's pink chaise.

"Pipes," Laura reiterated. Nodding, she knelt and reached a hand under the old-timey lounger as the Duke gave me a look.

I made my *what?* face, then she cleared her throat.

"We really do need to get moving, Laura." The Duke bent a little as Laura searched. But she wasn't searching. She'd gone very still. "Laura?"

Without another word, my CPS agent rose, her fist clenched around the pen, and then she quickly dropped it in her bag.

I looked at her.

"Lunchtime, then?" The Duke asked, brows knitting together. "I'll drop by the office?"

Laura's chest rose and fell like she was taking a deep breath, then she turned to the Duke with a bright smile. "One o'clock?"

The Duke nodded.

"I'll get my backpack," I said, not liking the sudden weird vibe.

I needed to talk to Delphine about all this.

Because I'd made up my mind. With CPS on the case, we were running out of time, and I had no options left.

We needed evidence so Aaheru would help. And that meant taking the chance and meeting with Anon715. Today.

And without another word, I turned on my heel and left the living room.

Chapter 16

School went by in a blurry fog. All I could think about was CPS, Arizona, the FBVA facility, and Mama. A knot of dread sat low in my belly, reminding me that life was a knitted sweater, and something had pulled at a loose thread, unraveling it stitch by stitch.

It was enough to force tears to my eyes. But I had to keep it together, because Delphine and I were about to walk into Chuck's Chocolate House to meet Anon715. I needed an iced hot chocolate to steady my nerves.

And Delphine needed blood. Lots of it. She was

so pale today, and there were dark circles under her eyes. But she said she was rationing the blood her parents had donated to her, until it was safe for them to donate again.

They wouldn't let her eat *any* of the organic blood she'd picked up from the blood bank on Saturday—just in case. Honestly, she might have to. I was really worried about her.

Plucking the hem of my black tee, I bit my lower lip as Delphine reached for the door.

I wanted to tell her to stop. That we should walk away. But we had no choice. *I* had no choice. This was our last shot. Because it was this, or give up and go to Arizona to Aaheru's safe house while my moms were taken away.

"Remember," Delphine said, pulling the door handle. "I'll look around and find them while you order a drink. If I pull my hair into a ponytail, you just walk out, and I'll follow."

Right. I nodded. That was the plan. If Anon715 didn't show, or if Delphine got any weird vibes, then we left.

"What are our names again?" I asked. That was

one of my conditions—fake names. It just felt safer—
in case things didn't go well. That way Anon715
wouldn't know who we really were.

"I'm Daphne, and you're Sara."

"Daphne and Sara. Got it," I said, taking a deep
breath as Delphine slipped into Chuck's. I followed.

Laughter and chatter echoed through the café,
mixing with the hiss of the coffee makers and the
clink of forks against plates. I glanced around.
Mostly high schoolers, some doing homework while
munching cake pops, others just talking.

Delphine's eyes narrowed as she scanned the
room, but I didn't wait to see if she spotted Anon715—
who said they'd be wearing a navy hoodie.

My heart raced as I got in line. There was only
one person ahead of me, and I hoped that was enough
time for Delphine to figure things out.

Pulling my phone from my pocket, I sent a quick
text to the Duke to let her know where I was, right
as the barista waved me forward.

I ordered my drink to go—just in case—and
when I got it, I slowly turned, my eyes drifting over
the tables until I spotted Delphine, slipping into a

booth opposite a person in a navy sweater with the hood pulled over their head. Anon715 had chosen a table near the back, half-hidden by a giant plant.

Delphine's hair still bounced around her shoulders, which meant we were doing this. My heart skipped a beat, and I took a deep breath before making my way toward them.

"Sara!" Delphine called, her eyes finding mine as I neared. "Sit, sit!"

She scooted over in the booth, and I slipped in next to her, my gaze on the person sitting opposite. It was a boy. Definitely a high schooler. Maybe a freshman?

"This is Anon715," Delphine said, waving her hand toward the boy.

"Just...call me Josh," he replied, glancing around.

"Thank you for meeting with us, Josh." Delphine took the lead, and I was glad. There was something about the way he fidgeted with his fingers, and the way he shifted on his side of the booth that made me nervous. "Josh was just about to tell me what school he goes to, as I don't recognize him."

Uh-oh. I mean, I wouldn't recognize anyone in high school, but because Delphine goes to middle school every year, she'd know him.

"You wouldn't. I go to Rexar."

"The *boarding* school?" Delphine wrinkled her nose and threw a look my way. Rexar Academy was a really expensive school about fifteen minutes south of Hopetown. "Well, that explains it."

"Look. I can't stay long," he said, glancing at both of us. "If anyone knew I was here, I'd be in serious trouble."

"Then we should get to it." Delphine placed a cool hand over mine, and I took a deep breath. "We need the proof. Whatever evidence you have that the FBVA are turning vampires rogue on purpose. Photocopies of whatever you have."

Silence. His pale blue eyes went wide as he cleared his throat.

"I thought you said you wanted to talk about what I knew?" he said, his auburn eyebrows bunching together.

"Well, yes." Delphine rolled her eyes. "But we have a situation and we need the proof."

"I . . ." Josh sat back in the booth and ran a hand over his hooded head.

My chest tightened as my pulse raced, and it hurt to breathe.

"Please." Letting go of Delphine's hand, I leaned over the table. "My mom . . . my *family* is in danger. We're going to be taken. We need to buy time so the Vampire Council can expose the FBVA, but their leader won't do anything unless we have concrete proof. We reached out to you because we thought you could help. That you *wanted* to help."

Josh's jaw clenched as he folded his arms over his chest. "Someone in your family went rogue?"

I nodded, and Josh sighed.

"That seriously sucks. The FBVA facility is no joke. I really, really wish I had something for you. I'm so sorry."

"So, you lied?" Delphine asked, her voice all tight and clipped. "Why meet with us then?"

"I didn't *lie*."

"But you just said you have no proof," Delphine countered, turning to me. "Come on, Sara. Let's get out of here. This guy's wasting our time."

"No, wait!" Josh exclaimed, as I scooted to the edge of the booth. I paused. "I want to help you, but I don't have a piece of paper with a confession on it. If I did, I'd have sent it to the newspapers myself. Whatever evidence you need is *inside* the FBVA facility."

"And you know this how?" Delphine scoffed.

He sighed and stared at the tabletop. "Because I do."

"Sorry, Josh. We've got to go." With a gentle nudge, Delphine told me it was time to get going, but I didn't move. There was something in the way he said it, all defeated and sad—like a balloon slowly leaking air. The same kind of feeling I had in my chest, as the hope there shrank away. He *wanted* to help us.

"Hang on, Daphne." My voice wobbled as I used Delphine's code name, and I swallowed the lump that had formed in my throat. "You have five minutes to explain, Josh."

With each thudding heartbeat of silence, Josh seemed to slouch farther back in the booth, until he finally dragged his gaze from the table to meet mine.

Raising his right hand, he waved it in front of his face, then shook his head, and I blinked really fast as the air around him crackled with static. The lines of his face went all blurry, and I held my breath. My moms had warned me about static and blurry faces. My heart *thud-ump*ed. Josh was using a glamour! And he was changing.

One second he was the auburn-browed, blue-eyed kid with a broad nose and thin lips. But in the next breath, his face changed. Still a kid, but his cheekbones were sharper, his nose hooked, his lips full, his brows black.

My eyes widened as I instantly recognized him. "Josh" was the vampire son of the governor of Pennsylvania. Delphine gripped my arm.

"You glamoured us?" she hissed. "But I suppose you're above the law, Simon Davis."

"I'm sorry," he whispered, and with another wave of his hand, his face changed back. "I couldn't risk anyone recognizing me, and I can't control it for very long. Here."

He dug into his pocket and pulled a card out of

his wallet. "ID. In case you think I used glamour just now to trick you into thinking I'm...well, me."

I looked at it. Yep. It was him. Simon Davis.

"Listen. I know for a fact that the FBVA are turning vampires rogue on purpose, and they definitely have a cure," he said.

"Oh? And how is that?" Delphine snapped. "I suppose your dear daddy, the governor, told you so."

He shook his head, then took a deep breath and pressed his palms against the top of the table. "I know, because...because *I* turned rogue. And I'm here, right now, because my dad made them give me the cure."

Chapter 17

His words knocked into my chest like a runaway truck. It wasn't possible. Nobody came back from being rogue. Right? I stared at Simon, squinting at his face as if I'd be able to tell if he had gone rogue and been cured. But all I could see were what-ifs. What if we could cure Mama? What if I could keep my family together?

"Nonsense," Delphine said with a snort. "Are you telling us that your father—the governor—*knows* what the FBVA is up to and is letting it happen?"

My eyes stretched so wide I thought they might fall out of my face. If that was true, then there was no way my petition to the governor would go any-where. It was a complete waste of time.

"Yes." Simon shrugged, glancing between us. "Listen, I know it sounds ridiculous, but it's true. I went rogue at school last year, and the FBVA were called. They took me away, and the principal told my father what happened. After that, Dad threatened to pull state funding from the FBVA if they didn't cure and release me."

"Umm...okay. But didn't all the kids at school know you went rogue?" Delphine asked. "How was this kept quiet?"

"I'm the only vampire student, so I like to take my meals in my room. I don't like being stared at while I eat...and that's where I was when it happened. The only people who knew were the teacher who came running with garlic spray—when I trashed the place—and the principal. Pretty sure Dad paid them both to keep quiet. Anyway, a few spritzes, and I was down for the count until the FBVA showed up." He said it all calmly, but Simon puffed out his cheeks and ran a hand over his hood. "So yeah. I know, because I went rogue, and was cured. That's why I'm on the forums. To let people know. But it's not like I have my medical chart or anything."

"Well." Delphine raised an eyebrow. "That all seems very..."

"Screwed up? Weird?" Simon nodded. "It was a nightmare."

"How...I mean, aren't you afraid of getting caught telling people?" I asked. If all this was true, the FBVA definitely wouldn't want the public knowing.

"Of course I am," he said, looking straight at me. "I mean, if they locked me up again, Dad would just pull their funding and pretend he knew nothing about it. He'd destroy them. But that's also why he can't shut it down, and why I don't want *him* to be the one who does it. The FBVA could destroy him too. It's an election year, and SynCorps—Bennington's company—is Dad's biggest donor. He's running for senator, and if Bennington cuts off funding for Dad's election, Dad won't be able to try and shut them down from Washington."

"Wishful thinking," Delphine muttered.

"Maybe...but he's going to try. He promised."

A muscle in Simon's cheek twitched. "You know, I wanted to attend Rexar because of their advanced coding programs. I thought it might be a nice distraction from the boredom of regular high school. To learn things I'd never had the opportunity to learn before...well, back when vampires weren't in the light." He glanced at Delphine, and she pressed her lips together. "My adoptive father has wealth and power, and he was happy to make that happen for me. He would do anything for our family, and that means protecting me no matter what. Even if doing so pushes us far apart. I'm so angry he's letting this happen to our kind, even if he'll be working on shutting them down once he's elected. So, yeah. I don't have my medical records...but I have this."

Reaching into his hoodie pocket, Simon pulled out an old, used blood bag—rinsed out, like Mama and the Duke did before putting them in the recycling.

"I don't know why the FBVA is turning vampires rogue on purpose," he said, sliding the blood bag across the table. "But I know this made me go rogue."

"We know synthetic blood is involved," Delphine retorted, rolling her eyes. "That's why we're here."

"No. Look." With a shake of his head, Simon pointed to the label on the bag. "This serial number. Specifically."

My heart thudded deep in my chest as Delphine plucked the bag to examine it.

"X-VMPR-3-1 compound S-Bag-Synth770. Origin, 001 HT?" As she read it out loud, Simon closed his eyes with a shudder. "This is it?"

"That's it. Any bags with that serial number turn vampires rogue. When . . . well, after I was back to normal, I overheard my father talking on the phone in my hospital room. He was trying to get someone to pull all of these bags from the banks, and it sounded like there were only a few out there as an experiment. But with so many turning rogue now—"

"And the new law that no longer pays human donors for blood," I interrupted, leaning over Delphine's shoulder to get a better look at the serial number.

"Exactly. It's out there now, and vampires have no choice but to eat it." Simon pointed at the bag. "I guarantee the bag your mom ate has that number on it."

"We have to check," I whispered to Delphine.

"Of course we will," she replied, turning to me with a sad smile. "But it doesn't really help us right now. We need proof so Aaheru will step in. I'm afraid if we show this to the Duke, she'd agree that this isn't enough. Without something that says 'This is the serial number for all the blood bags containing tainted blood,' it likely won't be enough for Aaheru to cause a stink."

"I'm really sorry I don't have anything to give you." Simon sighed.

"That's quite all right," Delphine replied, pressing her lips together.

"Anything helpful would be inside the facility," he continued. "Like, if you could get your hands on the actual antidote, that would prove they have a cure and aren't saving the rogue vampires. That would look *really* bad."

"H-how...," I began, then cleared my throat. "What if someone could get inside? What would they look for?"

Simon's eyebrows shot up to his hairline, and Delphine placed a hand on my arm.

"You can't be serious?" she hissed. I closed my eyes and breathed deep to try and slow my heartbeat.

"A cure is the only way to stop this," I whispered, slowly opening my eyes as I turned to look at Delphine. "I can't leave my moms here to be taken. I can't go to Arizona. And I can't end up with some stranger who wants to reconnect after abandoning me. This is my *family* Delph . . . Daphne."

Tears stung my eyes as she searched my face, the hard lines of shock melting to determination as she grasped my hand.

"You want to break into the FBVA facility?" she asked, and with each word my heart leapt farther up my throat.

"Wait, wait, wait." Simon leaned over the table, his eyes wide. "You have to be sure about this. If you're caught, it's game over."

But it was game over if we didn't. At least this way, I'd be doing something to try and stop it. "I have to try."

Silence fell as Simon chewed his bottom lip, and Delphine stared at her hand, the one clasping mine.

"Okay," she murmured, then dragged her narrowed eyes to Simon's. "You've been in there. You can help."

"Heck no!" he exclaimed. "You can count me out. I'm not ever going back to that place. It's awful. I was in the vampire holding cells, separate from where they keep the human families, and the vampire cells are these tiny closets. You can't talk to anyone. Can't do anything. I still have nightmares. I'm going to keep my therapist busy for years."

"Then you'll tell us everything you can remember," Delphine said with a nod, as Simon paled. "Anything that might help us...so long as you're comfortable, of course."

"I..." He trailed off, and I glanced at him.

"Please, Simon," I said with a sigh. "This is my *family.*"

Simon looked at Delphine, then at me, his jaw clenched and his eyebrows scrunched together.

"Fine."

My heart skipped a beat.

"But if you're going in there for the cure, you're going to need this."

Chapter 18

X-VMPR-reversal-3-1. Turned out Simon had found a discharge document on his dad's desk not long after he finally got home from the FBVA facility, and snapped a photo of the list of medications he'd been given. And since the serial number on the contaminated blood bags read "X-VMPR-3-1," he figured something with the same number, labeled "reversal," must be the cure.

All we had to do now was check the numbers against the synthetic blood bags in my refrigerator. Then we'd know for sure that we'd be looking for the right antidote. Only problem was, that bag of synthetic blood was in the basement, and so was Mama.

Well, no. That wasn't the *only* problem. It was the *first* problem. After Simon gave us the serial number of the cure, he told us all about the facility deep under the ground, and the guards, and the holding cells, and the lab, and . . .

It was a lot. My stomach bubbled all the way home as I breathed deep to steady my heartbeat, until all I could think about was all the things that could go wrong.

That we wouldn't be able to get past the guards.

That we'd get lost inside.

That we'd get caught.

That it would all be for nothing because we'd fail. . . . *I'd* fail.

When we got to my house, it was quiet. The Duke had made it clear that we needed to make sure everything looked normal, and that meant going home. Delphine's mom was worried about Mama in the basement, but our parents had decided it would be safer for me if Delphine stayed until the Duke got home —which would be in about an hour. Though right now, I didn't think Delphine could protect me from anything. She'd yawned at least three times on the walk here—and I'd never seen her yawn before. It must've been from the lack of blood.

But there we were, at the top of the basement stairs, my heart pounding so hard I saw stars in my vision.

There was no sound. Not even a shuffle. My eyes widened. Had Mama escaped? There was no way the Duke would have let that happen...right?

"Mama?" I called. Nothing. I turned to Delphine, eyes wide. "D, what if—?"

"No way." With a snort, she stepped forward and flipped the light switch. "The Duke would never leave her unsecured. We'll be quick. Straight down, and check the label. That's it. I'll stand watch to ensure your dear mama doesn't try to break her bonds."

"But...it's so quiet," I whispered. Something was wrong. Mama had spent all night slapping on the pipes. And then there was the banging this morning. Now? Nothing.

"I know." Delphine bit her lower lip, her pointier-than-human incisors gently denting the skin. "I'd do it myself but I'm so damn weak right now, and being around tar water will make me weaker. At least I can call out from the stairs if anything seems...wrong."

She reached into her backpack and pulled out a lightweight sweater, held it up to her face, and tied the loose arms behind her head to create a kind of eye mask.

"D, I'm really worried about this blood-rationing thing."

"It's fine, really. Mom's going to try and extract some blood for me tomorrow. Don't worry."

I pursed my lips, then took a breath, bracing myself to go down to the basement, but Delphine placed a hand on my shoulder. "I'm going down first. Even with this on my face, and weakened, my other senses are sharper than yours, and there's no way I'm letting you walk into danger ahead of me, in case something *is* wrong."

I swallowed hard, but before I could say anything, she started down the stairs, as if her eyes weren't covered to prevent the tar water vapor from causing a reaction. And for a second, I wished *my* eyes were covered too. I really hated the basement.

It was all shadows and dull light with boxes of old things piled everywhere. Mama called them memories. The Duke called them junk.

Each step we took felt like forever. I was still jittery from everything Simon told us, and wanted everything to stop. To go away.

"The protection circle smells intact, and I heard a shuffle." Delphine's words were breathy, and I glanced down the stairs, toward the back of the basement. *I* didn't hear a shuffle.

But Mama was there, just like she was the night the Duke brought me down to see her. Her hands and feet tied with garlic-soaked silver rope, smelling of pungent garlic spray, in a generous circle made of brick dust and tar water.

Except...she was out cold. She lay on the pile of pillows and comforter the Duke had carefully placed for her—there wasn't enough brick dust or tar water to make a circle big enough for an air mattress. My heart stopped as I looked at her, still wearing her ruined clothes, hair messy and knotted, skin all crusty with the Duke's dried blood. But Mama's blood too. She was like something out of an internet makeup tutorial gone wrong. They were tears. Dried tears.

And I couldn't help it. "Mama?" I whispered, leaving Delphine on the stairs as I stepped onto the cold concrete floor of the basement.

"Sophie, don't—" But Delphine's warning came too late.

I blinked, and Mama was on her feet, eyes blood-shot and wild as she opened her mouth. Then Mama screamed.

We both covered our ears as Mama charged, and Delphine yelled.

"The refrigerator, Sophie. Check the blood bag!"

But I couldn't. I was frozen to the spot. Watching. Waiting. Not that I had long to wait, because Mama ran toward the edge of the protection circle and bounced back into the pile of pillows. That was the effect of the tar water and brick dust. She couldn't pass the barrier, and when she hit that invisible wall, it was like she was shocked by an electric fence. At least, that's what the Duke had said. But there was something different about that invisible wall tonight. When Mama hit it, it started to . . . shimmer?

"*Now*, Sophie." Delphine's knuckles were blanched bright white as she gripped the rail, and there was a wobble in her voice that made my chest flutter, and my blood went cold. Delphine thought we were in danger. That meant we were definitely in danger. I took a sharp left and sprinted for the refrigerator.

Mama screamed again, and suddenly my fingers wouldn't work. I tried grabbing the fridge handle but couldn't get a good grip.

Handle. Grab. Blood bag. Phone camera. Click.

That's it. That's all I needed to do. I couldn't grab the bag and run, because there was no way I was coming back down here, and if the Duke found the bag missing, she'd know we were in the basement and were up to something. For this to work, she couldn't know...because she'd never let us break into the FBVA facility.

Behind me, Mama growled.

"The bag, Sophie," Delphine hissed, her voice heavy with fear, and that scared me. Enough to finally grip the handle and pull the door open.

A gallon of pink lemonade. A crock of butter. Five synthetic blood bags.

I grabbed my phone from my back pocket and started taking pictures. The white label was big, but the words were tiny, and my hands were shaking. One picture, two. I don't know how many I took, but better to be safe than sorry in case they came out blurry. I reached inside and flipped the bag over. Another label. More pictures.

Another bloodcurdling scream, and I sucked air in through clenched teeth.

"Got it," I called to Delphine.

"Get your human backside upstairs!"

She didn't have to tell me twice. I bolted for the stairs, and Delphine waited for me to pass her before following.

"Go, go, go," she urged, and I sped up. My heart pounded, and I felt sweaty, but cold. The kind of sweaty that made me want to wrap up in a blanket, even if my skin stuck to it. We scrambled through the door, and Delphine shut it behind us as Mama screamed again.

"Wh-what was going on with the protection barrier?" I asked, bending to catch my breath.

"That was bad news, Sophie Dawes." Delphine held out her hand, calm as a pool on a warm summer night, and that made me jealous. It wasn't fair that she was chill. Me, struggling for breath, and her acting like nothing had happened.

But vampires didn't have to breathe. They just pretended to . . . to fit in.

I watched as she removed the sweater from her face, as she stalked to the kitchen sink, as she turned on the tap, and splashed water over her face.

"A-are you okay?" I asked.

"I . . ." Delphine trailed off and rubbed a wet hand over her eyes. "Yes. I-I'm fine. Just making sure none of the tar water fumes linger. Did . . . did you get it?"

"Seriously, D. Something was wrong down there," I said, handing her my phone. "When she came at me, the barrier kind of . . . shimmered."

"I . . . I sensed an energy shift. As if the barrier is weakening." With a shaking hand, she took my phone and squinted at the screen. "I don't think we're in immediate danger. But a day from now, it could be a problem. You might want to tell the Duke. Just say you popped your head on down to peeka-boo when there was no clamoring, and a shimmery wall appeared. She'll know what to do."

I blinked, then blinked again as my brain worked real hard to figure out her words.

She glanced at me and gave a nervous chuckle. "You were curious and went down to see her because she was too quiet, then she pounced and everything started shimmering."

I nodded. I could do that. Definitely.

"Also, we need to plan." I glanced at her. "Look what we have here."

Delphine held up my phone, and I knew what it would say before looking at the screen.

This was it. I squinted.

> X-VMPR-3-1 COMPOUND S-BAG-
> SYNTH770. ORIGIN, 001 HT.

The same serial number of the blood bag that turned Simon rogue. We had a winner.

Chapter 19

We sat at the kitchen counter, math and social studies books open, half studying, half planning. Delphine insisted on making tea—to help me relax—but my knee still bounced as I chewed on my pinky nail.

"But how do we get in?" I asked. Because this plan was ridiculous.

"Glamour," she replied, filling in the answer to an equation.

"Delphine, it's illegal—" I began, but she cut me off.

"I know. I *know*. But I can see no other way to do this."

I bit down on my bottom lip. I couldn't either. It's not like two twelve-year-olds could just waltz up to a security checkpoint at night and ask nicely to be let in. Nodding, I looked at her.

"Okay...so you can make yourself look like someone else...like Simon did, and then let me in?"

Delphine shook her head. "That's not something every vampire can do. My power is different."

I was quiet a second, watching the way she stared at her math book. We'd never talked about her vampire power before. "What's your power, then?"

"The Elders call it emulation," she replied. "It's like glamouring, but it only lasts a little while. Basically, I can put people to sleep, and they forget what happened. So they wouldn't remember you, or me. Thing is, I can only do it to one or two people at a time. And—" Delphine broke off and glanced at me. "I can do it to cameras as well. I can make them go to sleep and stop recording when I go by."

"Umm..." My eyes widened, and my lips twitched. "That's actually super cool."

Delphine shook her head and smiled. "I'm glad you think so. Though it's been a while since I used it, so let's hope we don't run into too much trouble."

"So ... we're thinking the main gate only has a guard or two then?"

"Yes. Simon did say he only spotted one at the security checkpoint when he was leaving the facility. I could definitely handle that."

"Okay. And we take their keycards to get into the main building," I said, nodding. We could do this. "Right?"

"Bingo."

The rest of the plan was basically "wing it." Simon couldn't remember much about his arrival—because he was rogue at the time—but he did say the place we needed to get to was below the main building, and we'd have to follow the directory to find it.

"Get in, grab the cure, get out," I murmured. It sounded so simple.

"Correction. Get in, grab the cure, find concrete evidence that the government is doing this on purpose, *then* get out," Delphine said, her eyebrows bunching together. "The cure might help your mama, and your family, but we need to sound the alarm . . . if we can."

I nodded. Because people had to know the truth. That vampires weren't monsters. They were just trying to live their lives like everyone else. Whoever was doing this was the monster, and it made me so angry, and nervous. My heart raced. It was like a tornado in my chest, churning, getting bigger, putting weight on my lungs until my breath came in fast, shallow pants.

"Sophie?" Delphine leaned over and placed a cool hand on my shoulder. "Are you all right?"

"I . . ." I had to breathe and swallow down the anxiety. I knew Delphine would keep us both safe, and we'd do our best. "I hope we can find something."

"We will. Besides, I'd wager they never thought anyone would try to break in, so they won't be expecting it. That will work in our favor."

I was pretty sure a "wager" was a bet, but before I could double-check, the sound of keys opening the front door kept my mouth firmly shut.

"Calmly now, Sophie." Yeah, right. The Duke would probably take one look at me and know we were up to something. "You tell her about that protection circle immediately, though, you hear?"

"Sophie?" The Duke called, and my cheeks felt hot all of a sudden.

"In here, Mom."

"I picked up dinner," she said, entering the kitchen. "Oh, hey, Delphine. What are you two doing?"

"Homework," I replied, as she placed the fast-food bag on the counter. "Mom?"

"Yeah?"

"You might wanna check on Mama."

"I will in a while, kiddo."

"No, like, she was really quiet so I went down there, and when she saw me she ran into that circle barrier, but it was all glowing and stuff. Delphine says—"

"Don't go down there without me again." The Duke's brows scrunched into the *you're in trouble* face.

"I was just worried, Mom. I'm sorry."

"I was here, Mrs. Knutsdatter," said Delphine. "Would you like me to fetch our own supplies so you might strengthen it? It's really no trouble. My poor mother keeps that kit around, but lord knows if I went rogue she'd be deader than George Washington afore she got round to using it."

Maybe it was the way she said it, all flat and matter-of-fact, but I could almost feel the blood drain from my face.

"That's kind, Delphine." The words were nice, but the Duke's tone was not. It was her polite voice, the one she used to hide when she was annoyed. "If I have need of it, I'll call your mother. But for now, it might be best for you to run along home."

"Of course." Delphine gathered her books and winked at me.

The Duke nodded and crossed her arms over her chest as Delphine strode for the front door. At least she waited until we heard the front door click.

"Mom—"

"No, Sophie. No 'momming' me. That was *dangerous*."

"I know. I just... I miss her. And I was worried."

Sighing, the Duke dropped her arms. "I know, kiddo. And I suppose I'm glad you did, or I might not have known the circle was weakening. But don't do it again, all right?"

"Yes, Mom."

"Here." She slid the bag across the counter. "Cheeseburger and fries."

My belly rumbled, but I didn't think I could eat. It felt awful to lie, and worse knowing what me and Delphine had planned.

"We have to talk," she said. "Eat up."

Uh-oh. I grabbed the burger from the bag as she sat next to me. But she said nothing, just stared at me as I stared right back.

She nodded at the burger, and I sighed. One bite to get her talking. I could do that.

And it really was delicious. Okay. Two bites.

"I met with Laura at lunch. I think it went well, but I'm not comfortable about this morning."

Good. Neither was I. I took another bite.

"So, I made a call, and Delphine's parents are able to take you to Arizona tomorrow. First thing in the morning."

I stopped chewing, and she pressed her lips together.

"It's temporary, kiddo. Just until all this blows over. But if Laura came once, she'll check up again."

First thing in the morning? I swallowed the burger, hard, and stared at the Duke.

"Say something," she said.

I didn't know what she wanted me to say, but my chest was tight and the burger sat really heavy in my belly. This wasn't going to blow over. She knew I knew that, right?

"I'm not a little kid anymore, Mom," I blurted. Okay, so I was angry, and it showed. The Duke's eyes widened. "And I'm *not* going to live with strangers."

"Sophie, we've been over this." The Duke slid her hand across the counter, but I jerked back. She frowned. "I have to keep you safe, and this is how I'll do that. Aaheru's people will take good care of you, I promise."

Tears burned my eyes and I squeezed them shut. "You can't do this," I whispered, my voice breaking.

The Duke went quiet but scraped back her stool. It made an awful noise against the floor tile, like nails down a chalkboard. It was weird, because I normally kept my thoughts inside, always afraid they'd be too much for my moms, that something I might say would make them rethink adopting me—the Hoffs *had* handed me back when I no longer fit into their lives—but now I wanted to let my thoughts out. Maybe it was what happened with Simon, and the basement, and matching the bag numbers, but I couldn't keep them to myself a minute longer.

"If you don't love me anymore, just say so." There it was. My biggest fear. The tears came then, and no amount of shutting my eyelids would stop them. A weird sound escaped my lips, and my shoulders shook. Anger. Fear. It all poured out in thick sobs, the kind I could barely breathe around. And then the Duke's cold hands came down on my shoulders.

She kept them there for a second, then reached down and squeezed me from behind.

"Don't you ever, *ever*, say that again. Of course I love you, Sophie-Bear." She hadn't called me that since I'd first moved in with them—when I was seven—and it almost made everything worse. Sadder. "Do you really think I want you to go? I'm trying to do my best. It's not forever."

"B-but it is." It was hard to talk, but I had to.

"You keep saying it's not, but you're not listening. We sent that letter to the governor, together, Mom. You know if you go into that facility, you're not coming out. Not you, not Mama. No one comes out. Ever." Except Simon. But that was because his dad was powerful. She squeezed harder, and I turned into her hug. "I'm not going."

"You are," she said, kissing the top of my head. "Sophie, you know who I am. It'll take one call to my legal team and our arrest will make the news. This might be how we get it to stop."

"But you're gonna throw me into the boat to do it." There. I took her own story and threw it back at her. I said it, and meant it.

She stiffened and slowly let me go. But I wasn't done. "You don't want me here, because you don't think it'll work. If you did, you wouldn't throw me away."

I felt her step back.

"That is *not* fair." I had hurt her, but no one was more hurt than me. "My father threw me into that boat because he valued other things over me. I value you above everything. This is the hardest decision of my life."

I went still and turned to look at her. Bloody tears stained her cheeks, but I was too shocked to care.

"That's what *she* said in her letter," I said. The Duke's face twisted into a confused *who?* " 'I value you above everything, and giving you up was the hardest decision of my life.' That's what she said. Tara Washington . . . my birth mother."

She was quiet for a minute, then: "I'm sure she did. And I hope you *never* have to make that kind of decision, Sophie. Not the one I'm making, and not the one she had to make, because it's the kind of thing that destroys you if you let it."

I was going to get sick. I could feel the burger in my belly as it tried to come back up my throat.

I hopped off the stool and glared at her.

"Where are you going, young lady?" she asked, crossing her arms.

"To my room," I said. I started walking, almost stomping as I passed her.

"But you haven't even eaten—"

"I'm not hungry!" I'd never talked to either of my parents like this, but I was so mad. I passed the dining room and grabbed the banister.

I wanted to say something else. Something mean. Something that might convince her not to do this, but the chime of the doorbell screamed behind me, and I almost jumped out of my skin.

"If that's Delphine again, you tell her to go straight home. Because you're grounded, kiddo."

I made a noise in the back of my throat—half scream, half groan—and turned to the door. On tiptoe, I squinted through the spyhole, and the whole world fell away.

My palms turned sweaty, and my heart pounded until blood rushed to my ears.

I stepped back. Then again. Backing up until I hit the banister.

"Sophie?" The Duke asked, anger replaced with concern as she rushed forward. "Who is it?"

But I couldn't speak. That fluttering tornado from the kitchen started whirling in my chest again.

Because at the door was Laura, standing shoulder to shoulder with a man dressed in black wearing a bulletproof vest.

With the big white letters FBVA printed on it.

Chapter 20

W hat in the . . . ?" The Duke didn't have to finish. She yanked back the lacy curtain—one
of those fancy panels that kept people from seeing
into the foyer—and I froze. Two black FBVA trucks
were parked at the end of our drive, and a few agents
stood in front of them, gripping those scary-looking
guns that needed two hands to hold.

I whimpered, and the Duke turned, eyes wide,
her face paler than death.

"Sophie . . ." We were too late.

I was sorry. Sorry I'd gotten angry. Sorry about
the things I said. Sorry I was so hard on her. It was

different talking about doing something, but the FBVA was scary, and seeing them, I kind of wished I *was* in Arizona.

I grabbed her hand, and she let the curtain fall back in place.

"Mommy." It came out all whiny, and I *never* called her mommy.

She clicked her tongue and pulled me in for a suffocating hug. "Don't worry, Sophie-Bear," she soothed. "We'll be all right."

Then she wasn't hugging me anymore, and I felt alone and empty. I didn't even have a chance to say goodbye to Delphine. She reached for the door.

"Mom, your face!" It was still all bloody with tears, but she shook her head.

"It doesn't matter."

The door opened, and Laura did a double take when she saw the Duke.

"Oh—umm," she stammered.

"Ms. Snyder." The Duke nodded and glanced at the FBVA agent standing next to Laura. "Three times in one day. What's this about?"

"Are you okay, Sophie?" Laura asked, looking

over the Duke's shoulder at me, but I stepped closer to my mom.

"She's fine. We've just...It's been an emotional few days."

"I see," said Laura. And she did. She now stared at the blood on the Duke's face. "But I need to hear that from Sophie."

"I'm fine, Laura," I said, my voice tiny as another FBVA agent crowded the doorstep.

"All right. May we come in? I'd rather not upset the neighbors—"

"You bring armed FBVA agents to our door and worry about the neighbors?" The Duke's voice was like ice. "My daughter and I were in the middle of a difficult conversation"—she gestured between her bloody face and my probably bloodshot eyes—"concerning Mama, and you show up here again. With *guns*? You are meant to be Child *Protective* Services, Ms. Snyder. Sophie and I are grieving right now. Marie won't even return Sophie's phone calls. What, exactly, does the FBVA have to do with this?"

Laura cleared her throat, eyes wide with what I

hoped was horror, as she—fingers crossed—realized how scared I was.

"Sophie, honey, this is all just procedure," she soothed, bending so we were almost at eye level. "I know things are hard right now, but I need to make sure you're all right—"

"She told you she was all right this morning. And you and I spoke at length during our meeting." The Duke interrupted Laura and straightened to full height. This was the boardroom Duke. The Viking Duke. And inside, my fear turned to butterflies.

But Laura wasn't impressed. "And *I* did some investigating."

Oh...umm. There went the butterflies...and maybe the burger. I really was going to be sick.

"At around six thirty, night before last, a neighbor called in a community watch disturbance. Suspected domestic dispute, without specific location. A patrol car was dispatched and arrived at Freedom Row at seven. There were no signs of any disturbance on the street. Officer Manzetti remained on-site for an additional forty-five minutes and documented unusual activity at 617 Freedom Row." Laura pointed at the gold-plated house number next to the door. "They called us because they saw that the house belonged to registered vampire custodians of a human child."

Registered vampire *custodians*...of a human child.

I didn't care how scared I was. "You mean *parents*."

Laura glanced at me and nodded. "Yes, of course. That's just what they're legally called, Sophie."

"Go on," said the Duke. I glared at Laura.

"I came here yesterday. You were both gone. And then this morning...that banging. And this." Laura reached into her bag, and when she pulled out her hand, my eyes widened.

That night, the night Mama went rogue, she was holding a headless doll. But it looked like Laura found the missing head under the chaise.

"It was under that old couch." At least Laura had the decency to look sorry. I stared at the porcelain face of the doll's head, but she kept going. "These dolls are Marie's prized possessions, and I knew something was very wrong. And then those noises started, and you said you had a new air-conditioning system installed, and the work crew must have missed a connection. Well, I contacted the township, and there were no permits issued for a central air-conditioner install. Yes. It requires a permit, and the contractors would've had to file for one."

Not. Good.

I looked at the Duke, and for the first time since opening the door, I thought she might be scared.

"I made the call to the FBVA," Laura admitted, then looked at me again. "Sophie. Is your mama okay?"

"Y-yes. I mean . . . I th-think so." What else was I going to say? "Like Mom said, Mama isn't returning our calls."

Nodding, Laura pointed to the FBVA agent on her left. "This is Agent Rice. We want to rule out any possibility of . . . well. May we come in?"

No. No way. The Duke squeezed my hand, then leaned forward.

"Do you have a warrant?"

Laura blinked really fast. "I . . . no. Are you saying you won't cooperate?"

"Oh, I will. When you have a warrant." My heart thudded, but I almost smiled.

"We could get this out of the way right now—"

"But we won't. If you have cause, a judge will grant a warrant." The Duke moved closer to them, voice like ice, and Laura and the FBVA agent took a step back. "I'll have my legal team contact you tomorrow to negotiate terms of the warrant and its execution. That is, if you can get a judge to expedite. You have my number. Please inform me of a time."

"This isn't personal," Laura said, her eyes wide.

"Oh, I know. I *am* a lawyer, after all. Sophie's well-being is your job, but we'll be doing this the correct, and legal, way. Thank you."

And the Duke slammed the door shut.

Chapter 21

My bags were packed.

Some neighbors showed up when the FBVA left, asking what happened, and if we were all okay. Nosy Nellies hoping for something to gossip about, probably. But the Duke told them all it was a misunderstanding. That we were fine. That Mama was out of town and CPS was concerned about it. They were angry and outraged. Good. Let them. It was about time humans realized vampires weren't the bad guys.

After, the Duke drove me to Delphine's house pretty much in silence. That was it. She'd called

Delphine's parents maybe five minutes after slamming the door in Laura's face.

The first five minutes she hugged me tight and wouldn't let go. I think we were both pretty scared. But she called Delphine's mom, told her she needed help with something, and Delphine's mom told her to come straight over.

"What do you need help with?" I asked, as we pulled into Delphine's driveway.

"You leave that to me, kiddo." She parked, unbuckled, then turned with a sad smile. "You got everything?"

I nodded. I didn't really want to talk or say goodbye, or anything like that. Because it wasn't the end, whether she thought it wasn't "forever" or not. I didn't realize until the FBVA showed up how unfair I'd been to the Duke. She thought she was keeping me safe. Even tonight. She'd bought us more time so I could disappear to Arizona with the Abernathys.

And even if she didn't know it, she'd bought time for me and Delphine to save the day.

"I love you, Sophie." The porch light turned on as my mom, my rock, pushed a strand of hair behind my ear.

"I know, Mom." I sighed and threw my arms around her. "I love you too."

A shadow crossed in front of the porch light, and I pulled away from the Duke, her eyes blood-rimmed and sad.

"It's all right," I said, and she nodded as Delphine's mom appeared at the window, holding a plastic crate.

"Hey, Sophie," Delphine's mom called, sounding all muffled through the glass. I waved.

"You coming in?" I asked the Duke, but she shook her head.

"I'm not good with this kind of thing, kiddo. But know this. I would die for you, you hear me? I'm *not* leaving you. I'm trying to keep you safe."

Me too. I was trying to keep her safe too. But it didn't make it hurt any less.

She leaned in and kissed my forehead. "Go. Go on. At least you'll have Delphine to keep you company on the trip."

My throat felt clogged, sludgy, so I cleared it.

"You'll call me?" I asked.

"First thing in the morning, and as often as I can. The Abernathys will let you know if anything happens."

I nodded, tried to smile, then slid out of the car.

She popped the trunk.

"Sophie Dawes! Are you all right? I was about to send you a message through the interwebs when Mom got the call." Delphine. I turned around, a suitcase in each hand, and she ran toward me.

"I'm tired...but okay," I said, right before she squeezed the life out of me.

"You stay safe, Sophie," said Delphine's mom. I looked over my shoulder, which was a struggle with Delphine still hanging on. Mrs. Abernathy smiled and got into the passenger's side of the Duke's car.

"Wait!" I called, walking around to the driver's side. The Duke rolled down the window.

"Kiddo, no long goodbyes—" But I interrupted her.

"Vampire curfew, Mom. It's almost nine. Where are you two going?" My eyes slid to the plastic crate in Mrs. Abernathy's lap, and I could swear I saw a half-gallon-sized jar of brick dust.

"We'll be fine," the Duke said with a smile. "I'll drive safe. We're just going to strengthen the protection circle around Mama, and make one more stop."

"I'll be back soon," said Delphine's mom. "Mr.

Abernathy is inside making pizza for you. You girls try to get some rest. We have a long drive tomorrow."

Without another word, the Duke rolled the window back up, and I stepped away.

"Well, this just got serious," Delphine whispered, joining me as I watched the Mercedes roll slowly down the driveway.

This week, everything was serious. "I know."

"Mom told me we have a day before the FBVA comes back with a warrant, but she plans to be on the road to Arizona long before then. First thing in the morning. Did the Duke tell you?"

I pressed my lips together and nodded. Okay. This was it. "Which means it has to be tonight. Can we do it tonight?"

"We're going to have to." Delphine tried to smile, but her lips didn't make it the whole way, and I noticed how much darker the circles beneath her eyes looked. "Come on in. Let's get you settled. We'll wait for my father to go to bed, which should be around ten thirty." She put an arm around my shoulder. "You could nap until then if you'd like."

A nap. That sounded so good.

But my stomach growled so loud Delphine's eyes widened. I never did finish that burger.

"Or food. Let's get you fed. My dad's going to extract blood first thing in the morning, and I'll finish the half bag of blood I've been saving. It'll be a feast."

Oh God. The thought of eating brought back that really sick feeling. But I said nothing as Delphine grabbed one of my suitcases.

It was almost 11:00 p.m.

But I never did get that nap.

Delphine had one of those walk-in closets with enough clothes inside to open a store, but she had nothing suitable for a nighttime heist. Lucky for us, I'd packed a few black tees, black hoodies, and black leggings in my suitcases.

"Not my favorite outfit, I must admit," Delphine complained, pulling on the hoodie. "But I suppose it *is* comfortable."

"Well, we can't wear ballgowns."

"True." Delphine sighed, then glanced at me. "We're really doing this."

"We sure are. Do you have gloves?" I asked.

"Do *I* have gloves?" Delphine chuckled, opening a closet drawer. "I have an entire collection. Some of these are as old as, well . . . me!"

I grinned. Duh, she always wore gloves, but that's not what I meant. "Not the fancy ones. Like, ones I can use so I don't leave fingerprints."

"Oh." Delphine's smile turned to a frown as she glanced at the lovely laced collection. She once told me that years ago, girls and women always had to wear gloves when they left the house, and that's why she had so many—and why she still liked to wear them.

"I didn't think of that." Raising her hands, she wiggled her fingers. "Vampire. No prints. But I think I have something back here. They're winter gloves, mind. Heavy. Oh. When the Duke called, I took the liberty of extracting a bottle of garlic spray from our own rogue kit before Mom took it to help your mama. I figured they wouldn't need it for a protection circle. It's in the top drawer of my dresser."

"Will *we* need it?" My eyebrows arched. "There

won't be rogue vampires on the loose at the facility . . . right?"

"I would assume not. But you should take it. Just in case. Goodness knows that stuff would burn my skin if I tried to carry it."

Properly dressed and gloved—with a bottle of garlic spray shoved into my backpack—we waited a half hour after Mr. Abernathy went to bed before sneaking out the back door. Delphine had two old-timey bikes that she loved. Her parents had bought her one they thought she'd like—not new, definitely vintage. But it just didn't fit her style.

So, Delphine gave me a bike straight out of a whole other century with a crossbar and high handlebars, while she took the skinny-framed, antique hunk of metal she called her "absolute favorite." At least it wasn't squeaky.

My heart was in my throat as we left the house.

We'd just cycled past where the streetlamps ended, and it was so dark I could barely see Delphine riding next to me. We had no lights at all. Neither bike had headlights or reflectors, which was good. Two kids, bicycling on a weekday in the middle of the night? After vampire curfew? That wasn't suspicious at all . . . *not*. Without lights, we—hopefully—wouldn't attract any attention.

If we weren't riding our bikes, I would've hugged Delphine. Hard. *This* was friendship. *This* was family. Sticking together like glue through good times and bad.

"You okay?" Delphine whispered. We were mostly out of town now, with only a few dark houses for company on old Liberty Highway. Highway. I snorted. More like a twisting, turning lane. No road markings, barely any traffic. Lonely. Isolated. The perfect place to put an FBVA facility. "We're getting close."

"I'm good," I whispered.

We went silent, the only sound the *fa-zap* of our wheels.

There was no moon tonight. Well, there probably was, but clouds had rolled in, blocking it out, and my eyes slowly adjusted to the dark. Monster-looking trees lined the road, armlike branches held in the air, leaves for hair, and twigs for creepy fingers. It felt like they were watching.

An owl hooted close by, and my whole body shuddered with a bad case of the creeps.

Who-whoooo.

Another turn in the road. Another long stretch. Another turn. Another stretch.

Another turn...and then the darkness was bleeding.

There were red lights in the distance. Lots of them, and my heart dropped into my belly. It was the FBVA entrance checkpoint.

"There it is," Delphine murmured. And we rolled to a stop. "All right. You know what to do, Sophie."

I swallowed the hard lump in my throat.

"We can do this. For your mama. For vampires everywhere."

I nodded, and Delphine settled back on her bike before peddling. "Give me a five-minute head start, and then follow."

Chapter 22

With every pedal, my heart panic-fluttered. Delphine's outline had melded into the darkness by the time I started to follow, and I stuck to the tree-lined shadows on the checkpoint side of the road. *Pedal*. This had better work. *Pedal*. Because it had to. The low-lying branches hung over knee-high bushes, but those bushes soon gave way to a tall, smooth concrete wall. I was close enough to the entrance gate now to see the red lights of the security checkpoint glinting off the iron spikes at the very top of the wall.

There was no way anyone could climb over to get in.

Or . . . out.

For a place they liked to call a research and rehabilitation facility, it really yelled danger.

Pulling to a slow stop, I glanced ahead, and waited. I was a few hundred feet from the entrance now, where the wall curved away from the road, and the blood-like glow of red lights spilled onto the concrete ground.

"Come on, Delphine," I murmured, tapping my foot in time to my pulse. If everything went according to plan, she'd walk to where I'd see her and wave both arms over her head. If not . . .

A figure moved into my line of sight and waved its arms over its hooded head. My legs turned wobbly.

She was all right. Oh, thank goodness!

With a deep breath, I pushed off the ground and cycled forward. Step one, complete.

"How many?" I whisper-yelled as I got closer. Delphine grinned.

"Three. One standing at the gate, two more in the

little office thing. Here." She grabbed my handlebars as I hopped off the bike.

"Any trouble?" I asked.

"Nah. It was easy enough. I rode up, and the guard at the gate was quite confused—as expected. So I told him I was new in town and got lost on my way home from a study meetup. I asked if I could use their phone, he took me into the office, and I emulated them. They're sleeping now."

I nodded. "How much time do we have?"

"About an hour," said Delphine, reaching into the deep pocket of her hoodie. "Time for phase two. I got their keycards. Let me just get the gate."

As she disappeared into the small concrete hut, I rolled my bike up to the barricade. It wasn't just one of those long arms that needed to be raised for a car to fit through. It was about six feet high, with a shiny, reflective bar on top of two steel gates.

With a whir, it began to move, slowly opening into the FBVA facility grounds like a haunted door in a creepy movie, pointing into the darkness away from the entrance—one inch at a time.

I was so busy watching it, fear pooling deep down in my belly, that I didn't notice Delphine's return.

"I have a thrill in my old bones, the likes I've not had since my spy days," she said—and I jumped right out of my skin. "Let's hope that half bag of blood is enough to sustain my power, in case there are many more guards."

"Ohmygod." I inhaled sharply to avoid screaming out loud. "You scared me!"

She chuckled. "Sorry. Here. You hang on to these."

She held out three keycards, and I took them with shaking fingers. They all looked the same. Nothing printed on them. No photos, no words, just a black stripe. I popped them in my pocket.

"We need all three?" I asked as we pedaled forward.

"Better safe than sorry. One of these fine guards may have higher clearance than the other two. We don't know what kind of things we're going to find in there, and who knows who has access to what. It was the same in the Second World War. Different keys for different locks. I imagine these doohickeys are no different. Plus, I saw it on one of those detective shows my mother insists on watching."

Fair. We could use all the help we could get.

"Wait...you were a spy during World War II?" My eyes widened as we cleared the gate. And just in time too. The second we passed, it started to close automatically.

"Oh yes. If all goes according to plan tonight, I'll spin a few tales for you."

"Spin a few tales"? Maybe she meant she'd tell me some stories? But I didn't have time to ask. We pedaled faster, allowing the darkness beyond to swallow us whole.

The clock was ticking, and we had to ride our bikes like our lives depended on it.

Because they did.

We cycled down a long, winding road that cut straight through a forest. And there, in the middle of a massive clearing, was a huge gray building with two guards posted outside. There were signs to follow for parking, and building numbers, but Delphine told me to dump our bikes behind a bush while she took a few minutes to stand really still with her eyes closed.

It looked like meditation...but I knew it had something to do with her emulation power. Like, she needed to brace herself.

"All right," she eventually whispered. "I'm ready."

I followed her to the lobby building, and we just...walked right up to the guards. I mean, they yelled a bit, wondering where we came from. But then she raised her hand, and they...dropped. Like boulders. All crumpled up and just...wow.

That was so cool, I wished I had that kind of power!

"Can you make sure they're comfortable while I emulate this camera?" she asked, biting her bottom lip as she glanced at the security camera pointed at the door.

"Yeah, of course," I said, bending to pull one of the guard's arms from behind his back and then place it over his belly. I did the same to the other guard, until both looked like they were taking a nap.

That's when I straightened and glanced at Delphine.

"You doing okay?" I asked. She didn't seem any paler than when we left her house, but I wanted to be sure.

"Yes, I'm fine," she said, squeezing her eyes shut. "Let me just take a second here.... Why don't you use one of those keycards to open the door."

I pulled the keycards free and swiped one over the LED panel to the right. The light on the lock went green, and we stepped inside when the door slid open.

"What if someone comes looking for them? The guards, I mean," I asked, squinting as we stepped into the foyer of the lobby.

"Then we're in trouble."

My heart thudded in my chest.

Inside, everything was white. And shiny. Only a few of the lights were on because it was night—but it was still a lot brighter than outside, so it took a second for my eyes to get used to it.

A big white receptionist desk ran along the entire right side of the room, and on the other, a lounge area dotted with simple modern white chairs, glass tables, and fake trees. But it wasn't like the public could come here, so I wasn't sure who they were even for, or why they needed a receptionist area.

In the center back of the lobby, a huge metallic staircase ended in a landing before two other staircases split off on each side. Kind of like those old-timey rich people mansions in the movies Mama loved to watch . . . except metal. Cold. And prison-like.

To the right of those stairs was a wall of vending machines.

And to the left, a directory.

Delphine squinted as she looked at it. It was one of those big panels with a map like they have at malls, all color-coded.

I nodded, then pressed my lips together as I read the slogan under the big silver 3D FBVA sign on the wall behind the map.

WHERE HUMANS CARE.

I grimaced. "Which way? Let's go," I said.

"Hold your horses." Delphine grabbed my arm. Pretty sure she meant "hang on." "The research laboratory Simon mentioned isn't listed. Which makes sense, I suppose—as it's super secret. Okay. We should probably go here first"—she pointed at a big blue square in the map—"the records room."

"There could be another map there," I said, nodding. I pulled out my phone and snapped a pic of the map...just in case. Of what? I didn't know, and I had no time to think about it. Just like I had no time to deal with the anxiety brewing in my chest. "Come on, D."

And we ran up the stairs.

Chapter 23

Lucky for us, all the signs were color-coded to match the map, and it was impossible to get lost. We just had to keep following the blue arrows. It was weird. I thought we'd find more guards to emulate, but so far there were none.

"There it is. We'll need those keycards," Delphine said, picking up speed as I pulled the cards from my pocket. Sure enough, a big double door stood at the end of the hall, and I jogged to keep up with her.

I swiped the first card as we reached it. Red light. My eyebrows arched like the one fast-food place my moms refused to take me to.

"What in tarnation?" An angry V shape appeared between Delphine's eyebrows.

"Like you said." I grabbed another. "Clearance. Locks, keys. Looks like the records room is super important."

I swiped another. Red light.

"D . . . ," I said, my heart now racing. We couldn't have come this far to fail. There wouldn't be another chance.

"We're running out of keys." Delphine's eyes went wide.

"Last one." I held my breath, and swiped. Everything depended on it.

My future. Mama's future. The Duke's future.

The future of all vampires.

Orange light.

We stared.

"What does that mean?" I asked.

Delphine glared at the card as I swiped again.

Green light. "Aha!" Delphine shoved the cards in her pocket and looked at me. "This is why I hate all this technology. Silly things never work right."

I laughed and stepped into the records room before the doors had even fully opened.

"It's been ten minutes, Sophie."

I swear, she was worse than Mama hovering as I tried whatever she'd made for dinner. The records room was more like a server room. I'd seen them on TV shows—huge black boxes with hundreds of lights and buttons. There were rows and rows of them. But I was at the computer, well...computers. A whole wall filled with monitors and keyboards.

"Listen, not sure what you thought exactly, but I can search the internet, use social media, and do basic things, Delphine. This isn't a book or movie or something." The app on the computer looked pretty basic...but that didn't mean that it was. Black screen, search bar, plain icons.

Turned out we'd needed the ID card to even access the computer. At least there wasn't a password. I had my phone next to me, in case anything of interest popped up, but so far, it was a bunch of gibberish.

Delphine picked up my phone and frowned. "We have maybe forty minutes until those guards come to and raise heck."

"I know. I get it, jeez." As if I took my sweet time on purpose. I clicked on random things, hoping it would bring me to the right page. Nothing, nothing, nothing.

I used the search bar, and typed the serial number from the contaminated blood bag. Nothing.

I typed in "research facility." "Research lab." "Laboratory." Nothing.

Sweating. I was sweating, which sucked because the AC was on full blast, and I was clammy on top of everything. That's when the goose bumps broke out, and I rubbed my arms.

It was weird, really, to be in the FBVA records room. Like, why weren't there more guards? Were they that positive no one would ever try to do, well, exactly what we were doing?

Think. I had to think.

Guards *guard* things. Important things. If they weren't guarding here...then this building wasn't important.

I clicked out of the current page and pulled up the map directory I'd found earlier.

"What are you doing?" Delphine asked.

"Hang on. Pass me my phone." She handed it to me. I hadn't had cell service since we cycled through the gate, but at least the rest of my phone's functions still worked.

I'd taken a picture of the map downstairs, so I opened my gallery.

"Oh, *oh!*" Delphine bent closer as I held the pic up to the monitor.

"Follow the map," I said, pointing to the screen. There was the records room. I checked the downstairs map. It was there. And the lobby was there. I went through each section and matched everything on the screen to the photo.

"Sophie Dawes, you genius. This is exactly why we're an excellent team. Between my powers, and your brains, we will be victorious!" Delphine drawled. She pointed to a section of the map on my phone. It was a huge rectangle, almost twice the size of the rest of the building, with the words PARKING GARAGE printed on it.

I glanced at the map on the monitor. It wasn't there.

"Wait." Clicking back out, I typed "parking garage" in the search, and a CLEARANCE warning popped up. My heart skipped a beat, but Delphine swiped the card in the slot next to the monitor, and the warning went away.

"I think this is it." I couldn't tell if I was excited or scared, because it was almost the same feeling when the butterflies started. "D, this is *it!*"

OPERATION PARKING GARAGE
Classified Information

We read together. In our heads. Some of the words were too big or too weird when strung together for me to figure out. But I was pretty sure Delphine understood most of it. I glanced at the back of the office chair where she gripped the sides. Her fingers dug into the leather, and her knuckles were snow white.

"What does it mean?" I asked, looking at her. "They're keeping rogue vampires in the old parking garage?"

"And their families. They're calling it a parking garage to avoid suspicion." She said it stiffly.

"What about this part?" I asked, pointing at a really wordy part of the document.

"It means—" She straightened and cleared her throat. "They can do whatever they want with whoever is housed in that building—vampire *or* human. Imprison without cause, and experiment on them medically."

I swallowed. "Does that mean . . . wait. I mean, we knew it wasn't a rehabilitation facility, but . . . they're *experimenting* on them? Not just the rogue vampires . . . the human families too?"

My voice got super squeaky, but I was really mad. She nodded, and I pressed my lips together before glancing back at the document. Breathe. I had to breathe.

I shook, my hands, fingers, toes. Scream. I needed to scream. But I settled for taking pictures of everything. The Duke would know what to do about it.

Snap. Scroll. *Snap.* Scroll. *Snap.* Scroll.

"Looks like there's a map of that building attached at the end of the document," Delphine said, pointing at the monitor.

There sure was. I moved the mouse and lined up the shot.

Stabbing the screen of the phone with my finger, I took the picture, and scrolled to double-check that was it. Definitely the end of the document. Good.

I stood up and, without a word to Delphine, stormed from the records room.

Chapter 24

Thirty minutes. That's all the time we had left, and there was no way we'd be back in thirty minutes. We still had zero evidence except the pictures I took on my phone—which were a great start, but something the FBVA could just delete off their computer—and we had no antidote for Mama. I was really beginning to think it was all a big waste.

A big waste of time in a puddle of vomit. I was going to be sick.

We raced through hallways and down corridors, furiously swiping keycards every time we reached a door. But with the map from Operation Parking

Garage, it was easy to find our way to the heart of the real FBVA facility. Hurrying down six flights of stairs, we were finally in the right place—the laboratory and holding cells.

This was supposed to be a place where rogue vampires were taken and rehabilitated—taught how to be calm again. And their families were supposedly taken so they could be part of the recovery process. I mean, we had our suspicions. Delphine always said they took them so there weren't human loved ones causing a stink and calling the authorities. But the humans they took had extended family and friends that caused a stink every day.

"This way," Delphine said, pointing at the right turn ahead. There weren't any signs in this part of the building, just Delphine's map-reading skills. We ran.

"Ah, there they are, Sophie." It must be nice not needing to breathe. Delphine should've been huffing, like me. Instead, she could speak complete sentences, and before I could ask what "they" were, she raised her hand and knocked out two soldiers guarding a door at the end of the hall.

Not security guards. Not FBVA agents. Soldiers in camo. The real deal.

Wow.

"Must be close," Delphine said, slowing. Again, she snapped off all their ID cards and handed them to me. "The research laboratory is marked three doors down past this one."

"We got this." At least, I thought we did.

Delphine straightened. "Your show. You do the honors."

She'd meant using one of the cards she just stole, but an open door behind her grabbed my attention. I frowned.

"Check the map," I said, walking real slow toward it. "What's in there?"

"Umm." She squinted at the screen. "Administrative office, it says. Come along. Time is *not* on our side."

"One minute." I didn't know why, but something about an open door in a place where everything was locked down really made me want to go in and look around.

"Sophie—"

"One. Minute." I was real careful, and super sneaky,

216

but there was no one inside. It was a normal office. Bookshelves filled with, well, books. A desk, a lamp, filing cabinets, a potted plant on top, stacked trays on the desk, a chair, a painting on the wall showing a thin guy with close-cropped brown hair, holding a ginger cat.

It was Dr. Bennington. I remembered him from the photo we'd found online.

There was a computer on the desk.

I bolted to it, just to see if anything was up, and thank Chuck's Chocolate House...the screen was normal. It was a regular desktop. With no lock screen. Weird.

"Sophie," Delphine hissed. I looked up and was surprised to find her eyes wide as saucers. "Look."

There was a nameplate on the desk. Gold with black lettering.

Dr. A. Bennington.

"It's his office!" she said.

Even better! I pulled up the C drive and started looking at file names. Maybe there was something here.

I frowned. But there was nothing there except the files that came preloaded on every computer. Downloads, Desktop, Documents, Photos. I clicked through them all. Empty. Empty. Empty. Empty. That explained the unlocked screen. There was nothing on the darn computer.

Except photos. Two. One of a pampered kitty. The other, a photo of another guy posing with the same cat.

"Guess he likes this cat," I said, as calmly as I could, but I wanted to throw something. "That's all that's on here. Nothing but two stinking pictures."

"Is it a cute cat?" She was making fun of me now, I knew she was. But the smile on her face was genuine. She walked around the desk, and I clicked on the first photo.

That was the first time I ever heard Delphine gasp. Actually, no. It wasn't a gasp, more like the sound a dying alien might make.

It scared the heck out of me, and I whipped around in fright. Her skin was a weird color, beyond vampire pale, it looked a bit blue. The shadows beneath her eyes seemed even darker, and her lips made an O. There was fear—real fear—in her eyes.

"D? What's wrong?" I reached out to her, because if she was scared, I should definitely be scared. I'd never seen her like this before, and a chill wiggled up my spine.

She was staring at the photo of the guy with the kitty.

So I turned around for a second look.

It was a ginger cat. Yellow eyes. Shiny fur.

A normal cat. Actually...I glanced over my shoulder. It was the same cat as the one Bennington held in the painting on the wall. Maybe Delphine's problem was with the person in the photo?

I turned back to the desktop monitor. They were pretty normal too, for a vampire. Maybe the age my moms looked. Blond hair. White sweater.

"Delphine?" I was really confused. "Talk to me. What is it?"

"They had to pay the price," she whispered. Then her features slowly hardened from shock, or fear— whichever it was—to red-flamed fury. She repeated it again, this time stronger. Louder. "That's what he said when he...killed them."

"Who did? What price?" I asked.

Delphine looked at me, eyes wild but focused.

"Turn the room upside down, Sophie Dawes,"

she said. "If Bennington knows him, Bennington is likely close in age to the Duke, and I guarantee all his records are handwritten."

Ugh, of course they were. But it was more than that. "You know this person?"

She scoffed . . . well, snorted. "You could say that."

That was a yes, then. "What is it?"

"That . . . *abomination* . . . is the vampire who turned me. *That*, Sophie, is Asger."

We opened every drawer. Every filing cabinet.

"Our ally in the White House, indeed." Delphine hadn't stopped talking under her breath since we started our search. "If Bennington is working with Asger, there's an evil reason for it."

At least that was one thing ticked off the why list. I knew Asger was bad news, but he was supposed to be dead. Executed by the Council for turning Delphine.

There was definitely something really bad going on.

"The ledgers, Sophie. There on the bookcase. Start looking through them."

Delphine was chaotic as she flipped through

books and ledgers. Determined. Angry. She moved at vampire speed—basically a video on fast forward.

We were going to get caught. I was sure Bennington wouldn't have propped the door open if he'd left for the night. And if we got caught . . . we probably wouldn't make it out of here.

Okay. Calm. Deep breaths. Really deep.

Chill. Chuck's hot chocolate. Ice cream on hot days. Rides to school with the Duke. Mama's cooking. Love. Hugs. Safe. Relax.

I repeated that over and over as I scanned the bookshelves. If I was a crotchety old vampire, where would I keep my top-secret notebooks with all my evil things in them?

Think, think, think. I paused and slowly turned. Yikes. Bennington was definitely going to know someone was in here. Papers were thrown everywhere, and books lay open on the floor. All right. We'd gone into the filing cabinets. All the drawers in his desk—and yes, even checked for possible hidden compartments.

The potted plant. I walked over and lifted it off the filing cabinet.

"What are you doing?" Delphine asked.

"It's too easy," I said. "Why would he keep something super top-secret on a shelf? Nothing is locked. Not the office, the drawers, the filing cabinets. And there's nothing on his computer. I mean, come on."

"You think he keeps his records in *that*?" she asked, gesturing at the small pot in my hand.

"No. But I'm checking, in case." I ran my hand over the pot, even looked inside. Nothing but pot, dirt, and plant. Okay. "Check under the desk. Look for something small. Maybe something taped under there."

"Like a key?" she scoffed, reluctantly moving toward the desk. "A key to what, Sophie Dawes? There isn't a single thing in this room left unopened. This is ridiculous! And a *waste* of *time*!"

I stiffened. I'd never heard her raise her voice like this before.

"It isn't a waste of time, D. I promise. Let's just—"

"Bennington is working with Asger!" she cried, her whole face scrunching with anger. "This mission was doomed before we arrived. Don't you understand that?"

I didn't understand, because Asger was supposedly taken care of by the Council long ago. But

Delphine was hurting, and I couldn't stand to see her like this.

"I get it. But we need those ledgers, D. One step at a time. Ledgers first, then the cure for Mama. Let's just take a second and calm—"

"You don't get it. *My* mama is *dead!*" she exclaimed, cutting me off. "My adoptive parents will never be a substitute for her, or Papa. I'm not like you, Sophie. My birth parents were taken from me by Asger, and he turned me into *this*. I saw them die. But you? Your mother is *alive*, and you have a chance to meet with her, and maybe let her into your life in some small way. And instead, we're here, about to be caught by the very person who destroyed my world. I can't . . . can't . . ."

My heart leapt up my throat as her words stabbed through to my bones. Tears blurred my eyes as I replayed every single one. Her mother was dead. My birth mother was alive. And in between all that, I realized she thought I was ungrateful.

Swiping away my tears, I looked her right in her bloodshot eyes and pursed my lips.

"We're finding those ledgers, Delphine. I know

this is hard, and weird, but we could take them all down—Bennington, Asger, and whoever's behind all this. But let's get something clear. Mama, the Duke...*they're* my parents."

Silence fell between us, but we didn't have time for any of this.

"When we get out of here, I *promise* Aaheru will take care of this Asger thing. But I need my best friend right now."

She sighed, and her eyes met mine. "I-I'm sorry, Sophie. I think it was the shock of seeing him...and maybe using my power on a half bag of blood."

"I get it, don't worry." Scanning the office, my gaze landed on the cat painting. Hmm. I crossed the small office to inspect it.

It was an okay painting, but having seen photos of the cat...it definitely wasn't good. I reached out to touch the frame...and shoved it up to one side.

"Bingo," I said. Right behind the portrait was a little door. I say door, because it wasn't a high-tech safe. It was made of wood, and there was a keyhole on the right-hand side.

"You *genius!*" she exclaimed.

"Check and see if there's a key taped under the desk," I suggested.

Smiling, Delphine dropped to the floor to check under the desk.

"Nothing here," she said.

I shifted the frame back in place and scouted the room. The potted plant was out. Maybe the filing cabinet.

I opened the top drawer as Delphine ran her hand over the bookshelves and door frame. Nothing. Bottom drawer.

Nothing.

"D?" I asked, and she glanced at me. "It's not like we're going to spend time cleaning this mess, so..."

I nodded at the painting. Then jerked my chin when she looked a bit confused.

"Oh!" And that's when my meaning sank in. She smiled. "Sophie Dawes, I do declare."

And within seconds, the portrait was propped against the desk as Delphine used her weakening vampire strength to rip the old lockbox open.

"Jackpot," I murmured. Ledgers. Maybe ten. Delphine grabbed them all and opened the top one.

She had this vampire-fueled speed-reading trick that always blew my mind. Her eyes skimmed back and forth maybe three times, then she turned the page.

"Here, put them in my backpack," I said, yanking the straps from my shoulders. I tugged the zipper and held the backpack open for her to slip the ledgers inside. "All right. Let's get moving."

But Delphine just stood there, a cheek muscle twitching as I secured the bag.

"Sophie. I really am sorry," she said softly. It was the kind of soft that told me she needed a hug, so I pulled her in before she could tell me she was fine. "I know." I squeezed her tight.

Her arms tightened around me for a second, then she stepped away. Her eyes were rimmed with blood-filled tears, and my chest tightened. "You are my *best* friend, Delphine Abernathy. And now I have triple the reason to make sure we get out of here with everything we came for." I stepped back and breathed deep. My pulse raced as my heart revved faster than the Duke's Mercedes, and I just wanted to go home—to hide under my comforter and cry. Because my friend was hurting, and I didn't know how to help. I held up a finger. "Get the cure for Mama so my family is safe." Two fingers. "Get evidence to let the world know what the FBVA are doing." Three fingers. "Tell the Council that Asger's still alive and Bennington knows him."

Delphine swiped the back of her hand over her eyes and smiled. "Thank you."

"Don't thank me yet." I could be strong for her, because she was always strong for me. "We still have to find the cure and get out of here."

"Okay. We need to take a right out of this office," Delphine said with a sniff. "Let's do this."

"Lead the way."

I followed Delphine through the door. We took a right, ran down a long corridor, then took a left.

"We have to go through this place marked 'Operations' to get to the lab. It's the next one. On the right," Delphine called, right as two more soldiers turned the corner.

She held up her hand, and they both dropped to

the ground as I beelined for the door. It really was a neat trick.

I fumbled in my pocket for one of the ID cards and swiped. Green light. We quickly ducked in, and—

"God. Have. Mercy." Delphine's voice was barely a breath.

I stopped inside, Delphine right behind me.

It was a room the length of a football field, but narrow. On the wall to our right, a counter ran from the door we'd just walked through, all the way to a dark speck at the other end of the room. At intervals, there were swivel chairs and walkie-talkie stations, with massive TV screens mounted on the wall above.

To our left were workstation cubicles that also ran the length of the room.

"This is wild," I whispered, following Delphine as she stepped closer to the TV monitors. I glanced at the first screen and noticed it was split into six frames. All footage from hallways and the entrance lobby. It was security. "How big is this place that they need all these security cameras?"

"Not all regular security cameras. Look." Delphine

pointed down the row, but I didn't have vampire sight, and had to jog forward to see what she was showing me.

"No," I whispered, eyes widening as I homed in on the image of people sleeping in a dark room, the glow of a low lamp the only light. I counted ten beds, before focusing on the next frame. Also ten beds. And the next. And the next.

I hurried down the line of screens, and each was filled with images of these . . . dormitories.

"Snap a few photos, Sophie," Delphine said, walking around me toward the other end of the room. "I think we just stumbled upon footage of the incarcerated families."

Oh my God. I went hot and cold at the same time, and my palms got all sweaty. There had to be something we could do.

"Maybe we could try to free them."

Delphine stopped walking and threw a frown over her shoulder. "I wish we could, but we simply don't have time."

"What if we split up?" I asked, knowing we couldn't. Without Delphine, I'd be caught. I shook my head and fiddled with the hem of my black hoodie. We had to stick to the plan.

Then why was I so cold? Why were my hands shaking?

Probably because that could be me in there. And if I knew someone was here—right now—who might be able to set me free, I'd want them to try.

But I also knew our best chance to save them was to get the evidence we'd gathered to the media. And that meant leaving them here . . . for now.

Was this what the Duke meant? That sometimes people had to make really, really hard decisions, no matter how much they didn't want to?

A sob crawled up my throat, but I swallowed it down.

"Sophie?" Delphine urged, reaching out her hand. "We're almost there. I promise. The laboratory is through that door."

I nodded and forced all thoughts of the Duke to the back of my mind.

We had a job to do.

Chapter 25

Three long, shiny white tables took up most of the space in the laboratory, their tops covered with glass beakers and dishes, big mechanical boxes that looked like pressure cookers, and trays filled with glass test tubes. On the wall to our right, a counter ran its whole length, with microscopes, computers, and ... more mounted TV screens above. But this time, the people on those screens weren't sleeping.

I inched closer, squinting at the images as Delphine searched the lab.

In the first, a woman paced in a single room.

In the next, another woman, sitting on a bed, rocked back and forth.

Then a man, pounding the door.

"Delphine?" I said, pulling my phone from my pocket. I needed pictures of this too. "Pretty sure these are the rogue vampires."

I snapped a photo. And another. All while Delphine stared at the screens.

"Six...twelve...eighteen...," she counted, eyes welling with bloody tears. "This is an abomination."

I ground my teeth together as I tore my gaze from the footage. "Let's get this antidote, and get out of here."

Delphine nodded, clenched her jaw, then pointed to a pair of stainless steel double doors on the opposite side of the room. "That looks like some kind of refrigerator. See the thermometer at the top? I don't see anywhere else the cure could be."

It was definitely worth a shot. She started to move, sweeping around the long table closest to us before striding for the refrigerator.

"There's a keycard panel," she said, hand out as I reached into my pocket for the cards.

She swiped. Red.

Another. Red.

She swiped until we were all out of cards, and my stomach did a backflip.

"What do we do?" I whispered.

"The only thing we can," she said, shrugging as she bit her lower lip. "We already made a mess of Bennington's office. Stand clear."

She reached for the handles, and I took ten steps back, bumping into the sharp corner of one of the lab tables. I grunted with pain, but it wasn't sharp like I expected. What the...? Something at the bottom of my backpack took most of the impact.

"Three..." Delphine started to count down, rocking back on her heels as she got ready.

I slipped the backpack from my shoulders and circled the table, away from Delphine. Pulling the zipper, I reached into the bag, rooting past Bennington's ledgers until my hand touched plastic. I pulled.

"Two..." Delphine rolled forward onto the balls of her feet.

Oh. It was the spray bottle of garlic. I rolled my

eyes and shoved the bottle into the pocket of my hoodie right as Delphine called: "One!"

Boom!

The refrigerator doors came right off their hinges, and Delphine dropped them with a *thunk* as a wailing scream tore through the room.

"What in God's name?" she yelled.

I clapped my hands over my ears, and I'm pretty sure my soul left my body as bright white lights flashed over our heads. It was more like a siren than a scream, loud and obnoxious, and it fizzled through my pores like an electric shock.

I didn't think my eyes could get any wider. We'd tripped the alarm.

"That's our cue to leave!" she called, her frantic gaze flicking to the door. "Hang on!"

She ran into the refrigerator as I struggled to get my breathing under control. In. Out. In. Out. In—

"Got it! Quick! Your backpack!"

"You sure?" I asked, wide-eyed, as I pulled the flaps of my already-open backpack.

She carried a container—maybe the size of a lunch box. With a flick of her wrist, she opened it, and wispy smoke billowed out as she stepped toward me. "There were ten of these in there, and fifteen vials in each one."

Ledgers. Photos. Antidote. That *had* to be enough.

"LOOK." Delphine had to yell as the alarm sounded again, but she lifted one of the vials from the container as if it might explode. "X-VMPR-reversal-3-1. Says so right there on the label."

She was so excited. It was in her voice, and her eyes, and the way she couldn't stop smiling, so I smiled too. Then I looked. There it was. X-VMPR-REVERSAL-3-1.

It wasn't until that moment I realized something inside me was wound up like a piece of string, because it suddenly snapped, and my bones turned to jelly. Tears burned my eyes. I wanted to let the warm fuzzies flow over me, but we weren't safe. We wouldn't be safe until we got home. Until Mama took the cure. Until the Duke stopped yelling at us for being the worst—and best (I hoped)—kids in history.

"Now we've got to run." Delphine carefully put the vial back in the container, and gently placed it in my bag before zipping it up.

Oh my God. I couldn't think with all the noise.

The alarm paused long enough for a robotic female voice to say: *"Security breach."*

Then kept on going.

Bvuuuuuuuuuuuuuu. Bvuuuuuuuuuuuuuu.

"Ready?" Delphine yelled.

"What?"

"ARE YOU READY?"

I nodded.

She took my hand and laced her fingers through mine.

"DON'T LET GO, SOPHIE DAWES."

I wouldn't.

I couldn't.

It was time to run.

Chapter 26

We sprinted back the way we came, but this time, guards seemed to pour from doors and adjacent hallways, alerted by the alarm.

Delphine did her best to take them down, but after using so much of her energy breaking Bennington's safe, and ripping the refrigerator door, she was lucky if she knocked out one at a time. We *had* to keep running.

"Left, Sophie!" she yelled, yanking me. Her vampire grip was intense. I thought for sure she'd rip my hand off if I kept going straight, or ran the wrong way. That's probably why she kept yelling directions.

I recognized this hallway. We'd crossed from the converted parking garage to the main building a few turns ago, and were following the signs. We were near the records room, which meant pretty close to the staircase leading down to the lobby.

"Delphine!" I cried, as a security guard stepped into the hallway ahead. She raised her hand, and the guard went down, the thud of their body hitting the floor lost as the alarm kept blaring.

My heart was beating so hard I thought it might explode out of my chest.

"Nearly there," Delphine yelled.

"HALT!" The command came from behind.

I didn't even look, just kept my eyes on the end of the hall. The stairs were there, I was sure of it. Every step brought us closer and closer to the exit.

Closer to escape. Closer to saving Mama, and our *home*.

Yup. There it was. I could see the metal railing now.

I made my legs move faster, though my muscles screamed to stop. But we were right there.

Ten feet. Nine. Eight.

And then we were skidding. It was a tight turn, but we hit the top of the metal staircase at almost the same time, taking those steps like little kids smashing piano keys.

I focused on the stairs below me, making sure I hit every step.

I jumped to the lobby floor from the second-to-last step, and Delphine was right behind me. Okay. Lobby. We needed to get to the exit.

I looked up. Receptionist desk on our left, lounge area on our right, and straight ahead, a man standing in front of the door we first came through.

Wait, what? My heart stuttered and I came to a wobbly stop, complete with sneakers skidding against the shiny white tile.

This wasn't a guard. He took a step toward us, and my brain did a backflip as something slapped my memory. Where did I know him from?

Delphine's stop was a lot more graceful, because vampire...obviously. But when she saw the man standing in the way of our escape route, she pulled our still-joined hands, squeezed before letting go, then stepped directly in front of me.

239

"What are you doing?" I hissed, eyes still trained on the guy, still visible over Delphine's shoulder. He was dressed in a white sweater and tan pants with loafers. "What are you waiting for? Knock him out."

But Delphine didn't move. Not even a little. She was still as a statue.

"Now, Delphine. Take him down!"

There was no way a human could've heard me over the alarm, but he did. Or, I'm pretty sure he did, because he smiled, kind of. It wasn't a real smile. Just an *I got you* lift of the lips that sent ice cubes up my spine. The same smile I'd seen earlier tonight. And then it hit me. It was Bennington.

Well, crap. My tongue felt like sandpaper as I tried swallowing the lump in my throat.

And what was that in his hand? I squinted over Delphine's shoulder. It looked like one of those slide-show clickers our teachers used at school.

He raised it up next to his face, clicked it, and just like that, the alarm died mid-siren.

Thank goodness. Except it didn't stop in my head. My ears thudded loudly, mixing with a left-over dizzy *whomp* I'd be hearing for days.

"Ah," Bennington said. "So much better, don't you think?"

Delphine didn't move, or say anything, and that made my breathing all fast and heavy. I mean, it was anyway from running, but now it was different. Like some invisible giant squeezed my lungs and I couldn't get enough air.

"Tell me, girls. Did you find whatever it is you're looking for, or do these gentlemen need to give you a...tour...of the facility?"

Huh. He had a weird accent. It sounded a bit like the Duke's, but I only heard hers when she said certain words. She'd lived in so many countries that I supposed 1,200 years of wandering the world would erase anyone's accent. But his...It was thicker, and reminded me of those few times the Duke slipped back to her Scandinavian roots.

I wished that was all my ears picked up. Boots, lots of them, thundered on the landing behind us, and I whipped around, eyes wide. Security guards. Delphine turned, hand raised, but before she could do whatever it was she did, fingers gripped her wrist.

An *eek* came from one of us—my money's on me—as I realized Bennington just poofed next to us.

"Now, now," he said, smiling down at Delphine. His eyes never left her. "You know better than that, my dear."

Delphine kept her mouth shut, but I saw her stiffen, and something like rage twisted her face.

"Do it!" I exclaimed.

"Oh, but she can't. You can sense it, can't you, Delphine?" he chuckled, and my eyes widened as he closed his. A ripple rolled over his skin, then it shimmered as his cheekbones seemed to move higher. His lips stretched wider. His nose changed shape. He opened his eyes and smiled. "I sired her, you see. And in her weakened state, there's no way she could overcome me. I'll need my ledgers back, of course. And the reversal serum. You forgot to emulate the cameras in my office...and the laboratory." He winked, and my heart raced as I squinted at him. Bennington wasn't *working* with Asger; Bennington *was* Asger! Bennington was using a glamour.

"But tell me," he continued, staring down at Delphine. "Why, after all these years, would my old progeny come calling? I think, perhaps, this was a case of two child vampires going rogue. Two more for my collection. An apt punishment for thieves."

That was it. Delphine might be happy to stay quiet, but I couldn't bite my tongue. "Nice try, *Asger*, but I'm not a vampire. And everyone in my school knows that, so no one will believe you."

His watery blue gaze shifted to me, and he chuckled. The sound of it made my stomach churn.

"But the press will believe whatever I tell them, little one. They always do. And it will get reported exactly as I say, so your little friends and teachers will start to wonder if they were wrong all along." He tilted his head. "Do your parents know you're here?"

Good. If I kept his attention on me, maybe Delphine would figure out a way to wriggle out of this. She was three hundred years old for crying out loud. She could figure it out, right? But she turned a little and mouthed an overexaggerated *no*. No. As in... stop talking? As in, leave it to her?

But that's when the little hairs on my arm stood on end, because I got a real good look at her face. It wasn't scrunched up with anger; it was scrunched up with fear. Paralyzing fear. Oh my God. Delphine was *scared*.

Crap. I had to think, fast, because it looked like getting out of this was left all up to me.

"Yes," I replied, locking eyes with the guy who turned my best friend into a vampire after killing her birth parents. Right. In. Front. Of. Her. "They know exactly where we are, actually."

"Wonderful. Then they'll come looking for you both, and you'll be reunited soon."

That sick son of a slug butt! We were going to get out of here, because I was angry now, and I felt the weight of everyone needing me settle on my chest. Mama. The Duke. Delphine. But it wasn't just them, it was vampires everywhere. They took a big risk walking into the light, letting the world know they were real, trusting humans to accept them. Then the whole turning rogue thing scared people and made them treat vampires differently. But now we had the proof we needed to make sure the world knew that vampires weren't to be feared. They were just like humans—some were good, and some were bad.

"It's fortuitous that you're here," Bennington—*Asger*—said, smiling. "I do love juvenile test subjects. Far more vicious than their adult counterparts. I think I'll transform your little human friend into a vampire first, then turn you both rogue at the same time to study the results.

"I always thought you'd make a wonderful soldier, Delphine," he continued. "An army of supercharged vampires marching on the government. Think of the *glory* it would bring—a happy Council, vampires in power. It will exonerate me in the eyes of the Ancients."

Oh. My. God. "You're turning them rogue...so you'll have an *army*?" I exclaimed, balling my fists. This guy was...was...*evil*.

Asger chuckled as his eyes slid to mine. "Oh, dear child. A handful of rogues does not an army make. Why do you think we take the families? We turn them first, *then* administer the rogue serum. And now that I've discovered how to control my new family, the time is right to distribute the serum across the country. You'll both make fine additions to our cause."

Heat flooded my veins and I wanted to scream, but a flicker out of the corner of my eye reminded me that the guards were slowly coming down the stairs. All it would take was a distraction.

We were going to get out of this. We *had* to.

"There's just one small problem with that," I said, stepping closer to Delphine. This time, I smiled at him, and hoped maybe that smile would give him a strong case of the oh-nos. "See, we already sent photos of some interesting pages in your ledgers to the authorities, so it doesn't matter what you *say* you're going to do, because you're going down."

Okay, so we hadn't, because I hadn't been able to get a cell signal, but *he* didn't know that. I tipped my chin as he narrowed his eyes.

"No. You didn't have time to do that." He shook his head, but I arched an eyebrow.

"Want to bet? *And* your little security cameras don't cover every inch of every room. I had plenty of time to snap photos while Delphine was dealing with the refrigerator door." I smiled.

"Why you little—" He let go of Delphine and lunged for me.

"Now, D!" I yelled, slipping my hand into the pocket of my hoodie.

I couldn't tell if she hesitated or not, because my eyes were on Asger as he grabbed me by the shoulders.

But I was ready for him.

I pulled the garlic spray from my pocket and aimed it right at his face.

"Night night, Asger," I said, and his eyes widened.

I thought the sweetest sound might be the thud of the guards dropping on the stairs as Delphine emulated as many as she could. But it wasn't.

It was when I pulled the spray trigger, and Asger woke the night with his screams.

Chapter 27

We ran. I couldn't believe we were free of the facility, but we weren't safe yet.

Push. I had to push. Every breath, every step, took us farther from the facility, and we had no time to lose. How long did we have until Asger followed? Because, he would follow . . . or send soldiers after us at least.

Thank goodness for the garlic spray—even if it wouldn't keep him down for long. Just enough to give us a good head start.

"Are. You. Okay?" Man, I was out of breath, but Delphine didn't answer, which wasn't fair, because she didn't, well, breathe.

She reached our hidden bikes first, grabbed hers, then waited for me to grab mine. But I was too busy gulping air.

"Thank you," she said at last. I looked at her. She was already getting on the bike.

I nodded but didn't feel right about her thank-you. Her eyes were rimmed with blood, and I bit my bottom lip.

"D," I began, with no idea where I wanted it to go . . . but we had to get moving. *Now.* "Thank *you* too. You kicked butt in there."

Nodding, she started pedaling down the winding drive toward the main entrance gate, and I pushed off two seconds after her.

"Thanks." Her voice was quiet, without any of the usual Delphine-ness. I wanted to ask what was wrong and how I could fix it, but not here. We had to concentrate.

I pedaled hard to keep up.

The night was still dark, even if it felt like we were inside for hours.

And that's when shouts rang out behind us, nearly drowned out by the roar of my pulse.

We veered into the woods the second we heard those shouts, but neither bike was meant for off-roading. It was bumpy as all heck, even though we found an old walking path to cycle on.

No vehicles passed us on the main drive, and no boots crashed through the forest floor behind us. Where were they?

"Up ahead," Delphine said.

I followed her gaze and pedaled even faster. Red lights winked through the darkness. The entrance checkpoint.

I didn't want to say so, but something didn't feel right. Delphine must've felt it too, because she slowed down.

"Whatever happens at the checkpoint, Sophie, you keep going." She rolled to a stop, and I skidded to a halt.

"What are you doing?" My brows knitted together. "What do you mean, whatever happens?"

"You just keep on pedaling and make a beeline for home."

That awful feeling in my stomach came back. "But with you."

"Sophie—" The way she said it, all *someone give me strength*. I cut her off.

"No, Delphine. We go home together." It was one thing to decide to abandon all those people, but another to abandon Delphine. I knew what she was saying. My backpack had the antidote and the ledgers inside. She thought she wouldn't make it and wanted to make sure I got away so I could make things happen. "No way. I'm not leaving you."

She didn't say anything, and I could barely see her face, but I took her silence for okay.

Good.

"Do you have a signal on your cellular device yet?" she asked.

I dug into my pocket and pulled out the phone. Nada. I shook my head. "I have a case of the creeps, like we're being watched," I said.

"One hundred percent. Keep your wits about you, Sophie Dawes." Delphine pushed the pedals of her bike but threw a hooded look over her shoulder.

251

"You are the best friend I've ever had. In all my three hundred years."

It was probably the doomy atmosphere, and the sinking feeling, because those words punched me right in the stomach.

And I had to tell myself not to cry.

We carefully pedaled from the woods onto the main road, maybe two hundred feet from the checkpoint.

It was . . . quiet. Too quiet.

I didn't have really sharp eyesight like Delphine, but I tried anyway to see if the guards had woken up and were waiting for us.

"Any sign of anyone?" I whispered, but Delphine shook her head.

"I can't smell the guards," she whispered back. "There's a trace, but they've been gone awhile."

We slowly rolled toward the guard house, and my skin fizzed with electricity as the dull red lights did their best to brighten the darkness. But they couldn't.

I kept a close eye on Delphine. Every twitch

she made. Every tilt of her head. She was watching. Listening.

She stopped her bike, so I did the same.

"There isn't a soul here," she murmured. "Stay put, Sophie. I'll go into the office and open the gate."

But that's when Asger's voice rang out in the darkness. "I think not."

My heart almost exploded in my chest. Eyes wide, I turned around, but there was nothing there. Nothing and no one.

"Sophie..." The wobble in Delphine's voice sent all the blood in my head straight to my toes. It happened so fast that by the time I'd turned around to the checkpoint again, I had to grab on to the handlebars to keep upright.

But that was nothing. It was like my body wanted to distract me, to keep my mind busy so I wouldn't freak out. Because standing right there, on our side of the checkpoint barrier, was Asger. He just... appeared. And his glamour was back in place. When we ran from the building, he was Asger, but now he was Dr. Bennington once more.

"Clever girl." His words were calm, but the dull

red glow of the lights fell across his face, darkening hollows and shadows so he looked all twisted with anger. There was a cloth in his hand. He raised it, and dabbed at his eyes as I dipped my hand into my pocket.

Because it didn't matter if I was scared out of my mind. We were getting out of here, and I'd use that garlic spray again if I had to.

"I wasn't prepared before, but I am now. My, my. What ferocity."

He looked right at me, but I didn't jerk back or shrink into myself. I was the daughter of Freyja Knutsdatter and Marie Dawes. Instead, I straightened my shoulders and glanced at Delphine.

This time she found her voice.

"My friend told the truth before," she said, putting on her best *excuse-you* drawl. "The information has already been sent to the media via cellular device. So, stand aside, sir, unless you wish to make matters worse."

"Stand aside?" He chuckled and moved toward us, carefully, eyes darting between me and Delphine. "Why, my dearest Delphine, you offend me. We're all going to calmly stroll back to my office and have a civil conversation. Because you know as well as I that you're bluffing."

That's when I heard it, the sound of boots and metal storming out of the woods onto the paved road behind us. Because... of course. I didn't even have to look, but I threw a glance over my shoulder anyway. Yep. Armed soldiers. And I was all out of sweaty palms for the night. Enough was enough.

I turned back and narrowed my eyes, ready to... well. I'm not sure what I was ready to do, but I would fight if I had to.

And so would Delphine. That scared vampire from the lobby was gone. *This* was my best friend in the whole world, and in true Delphine style, a strange half smile pulled at her lips.

My mouth went dry as I fought the go-Delphine-go in my throat. He was in for it.

She raised her hand—yes!—and blasted Asger with her emulation.

His eyes widened, and he froze, but he didn't go down like the human guards and soldiers. It was as if Delphine molded an invisible barrier around his body, and he had trouble moving against it. He looked like a mime in slow motion as he struggled to step forward.

"Pedal, Sophie." Delphine's yell caught me off guard. Not only because I was in an Asger's-all-stuck trance, but I wasn't going without her. We'd already covered that.

"No way," I said, turning to her, but she was . . . gone. What the . . . ?

Then a muffled yell from inside the guard house. "It won't last for long!"

That's when the checkpoint gate began to open, reaching toward me, beckoning me to flee. And she was there, on the other side of it, eyes wide with a *get moving* look.

Together. We would leave together.

Body jolting, my pulse spiked into high gear, and I pushed the bike's pedals like I was on fire.

Which must've sent warning bells through the soldiers behind us, because those boots chewed up the road like thunder rattling old windows.

Go. Go. Go. I chanted with each pedal, eyes focused on Delphine. On her nod of approval. On her getting ready to push her own pedals when I reached her. On her eyes widening. Her mouth opening. On her earsplitting scream. *"SOPHIE!"*

I didn't even have time to react as hands clamped down on my shoulders. One second, I was riding the bike, the next, I was upright, sneakers on the ground with my arms yanked behind my back by a single large hand.

"Foolish!" Asger was angry, really angry, his touch so cold I thought my wrists would freeze through. I barely noticed the slowing of the boots behind us, but at some point, they stopped their forward march.

"Let me g " I screamed, but he stopped that really quick by covering my mouth with his other hand. My eyes widened.

"I have tried to be *reasonable*," he growled, but he wasn't talking to me. All his focus was on Delphine. "I asked you to join me all those years ago, and you refused."

"You're supposed to be dead!" Delphine's words rang out clear and loud as she got off her bike. It dropped as she took a step toward us.

"Go, Delphine!" I yelled, or tried to. It was hard to yell with some vampire dude's hand over my mouth. But she still knew what I was trying to say.

"I can't," she replied, not looking at me, but Asger. And I knew why. The backpack. I had everything we needed, and she'd thought she could at least get me away. "Take me, Asger. She has nothing to do with this."

"I beg to differ. If you think I'm going to let either one of you leave, you're sadly mistaken. I've worked too long and too hard to let you destroy my plans. Remind me to add new anti-vampire security measures, would you, my dears?"

"She's just a human kid. No one will listen to her," said Delphine. "Take me."

Laughing, he loosened his grip on my hands, but not enough for me to get free.

"Yet you seemed so confident earlier. So certain of your evidence. Come now. Don't be silly. Those soldiers are armed, Delphine. If either of you try anything, they will shoot to kill, on my order. That wouldn't bode well for your . . . friend."

"What soldiers?" Delphine asked, squinting into

the darkness behind us. "You're getting senile in your old age, Asger. There's no one there."

Was this a distraction? I stared at Delphine and waited for her to mouth something, to tell me what she wanted me to do. Because I'd heard them. I saw them. There were definitely soldiers.

Asger scoffed but turned us to the side so he could check.

And my eyes widened. Behind us, the wall of soldiers was crumpled on the ground.

"How—?" Asger began, and I felt a ripple of rage go through his cold body.

"I would suggest"—another voice rang out in the darkness, near Delphine, and my lungs stopped working for a whole ten seconds; it sounded like . . . but it couldn't be—"letting go of that child."

That was enough for me. I bit down on his hand and barely had time to turn my head before something was tossed in the air, through the open gate.

Before Delphine caught it.

Before I realized what it was. A small crossbow.

Before she drew back the firing wire.

Before she shot it.

And hit him.

In the shoulder.

As he roared, he released me, and I started running.

Another arrow clicked into place, and another shot rang out.

More roars.

Another arrow.

Another roar.

It wasn't until I neared Delphine that I realized I was crying, that hot, salty tears streamed down my cheeks.

Not until a figure separated from the darkness.

A tall figure. An adult figure.

And as they held their arms wide open, I knew.

I'd never been so relieved in my life as I slammed into the Duke's waiting arms.

Chapter 28

Aahcru will have to deal with him," said the
Duke.

"He's not dead?" I asked.

"Since it appears he's the cat with nine lives, certainly not," said Delphine.

I didn't care how my mom was here, I was just
happy she was. I stood there, safe in her arms, as
we all kind of stared at Asger's limp body. Delphine
had shot three arrows, and all three hit him. But
the arrows were wooden, and I knew, even before I
asked, that they wouldn't really kill him.

"What happened to the soldiers?" I asked.

This time the Duke spoke, her voice calm and gentle as she stroked my hair. "I took care of them. My power is a slightly different version of Delphine's—succumbing. I can just focus and put large numbers of humans to sleep."

Wow!

"We've got to get moving," she said. "Come on. The truck's over here. We just have to be careful, kiddo. It's hours past curfew."

"Mom?" I asked, and she glanced down at me. I didn't even question what truck she was talking about. No one we knew had a truck. "Thank you."

Pressing her lips together, she gave me a "look." "You're welcome, but you and I have to have a very long talk, young lady...after I hug you senseless. Mama would kill me if anything happened to you. Don't ever do anything like this again!"

I should've been scared, but instead I smiled. Because my moms loved me, and I loved them. We were family, and nothing was going to separate us.

We had the cure, we had evidence...and everything was going to be fine.

Turned out the truck was one of those white rent-a-trucks with a logo down the side. The ones used for moving to a new house.

"What's this?" I asked, brows knitting together.

"You weren't the only ones with a plan tonight." The Duke scoffed as she waved into the cab of the truck. "Though ours certainly didn't involve breaking into a top-secret government facility."

"Ugh," Delphine groaned, as the driver—because there *was* a driver—rolled down the window.

"Delphine Antoinette Helene Marie Bouvier Abernathy!" Uh-oh. My eyes widened. "You get your butt into the back *immediately*, you hear me?"

"Yes, Mom."

"There I am, doing my darnedest to help our friends, only to get home—after driving *all* the way to Allentown for this rental—to find the garlic spray missing from our kit, and find *neither* of you at home! How *dare* you leave the house in the middle of the night!" Delphine's mom opened the door of the truck, her face flushed, her eyes tear-stained, and hopped out. "What were you *thinking*?"

Without another word, Delphine's mom stepped forward and tugged Delphine into a bone-crushing hug. "Don't you *ever*"—she kissed her head—"*ever*"—another kiss—"do that again! You hear me?"

"Mom..." Delphine's voice broke, and she tightened her arms around her mom's waist. "I'm so grateful you found my note—"

"You won't be grateful when we get home, ma'am!" Delphine's mom snapped, pulling away, before turning to get back in the truck. She paused. "I love you. Now, let's get moving."

Delphine cringed, and I sucker punched her arm.

"Ow!"

"You left a *note*?"

"Yes! Just in case something went wrong. And it *did*!" Delphine rubbed her arm, and I smiled really big.

"I'm really, really glad you did."

"Come on, you two," said the Duke, appearing behind us. "Load up."

"In the back?" I asked, turning.

"In the back. Mrs. Abernathy will drive in case we're pulled over. Then you can tell us what happened and whatever possessed you to do something so dangerous." The Duke glanced between us, then settled her gaze on Delphine. "And how you know Dr. Bennington."

"That's a long story," Delphine said with a snort.

"We have all night." The Duke walked around us and held out her hand. "Time to go."

Delphine filled in the Duke on who Bennington really was, and then we told her everything. Everything from meeting Simon, to the basement, to our plan, to the facility. By the end, the Duke and Delphine's mom were very quiet, and I was pretty sure I'd be grounded for a whole year. Maybe more. Maybe all through high school too.

"What about ... this?" Delphine asked, gesturing at the van. We sat on a narrow bench behind the driver and passenger seats, strapped in with really tight seat belts. It wasn't exactly a comfortable ride. But good question and good idea—distract my mom.

"I thought we might be able to get your mama into the truck and move her," the Duke said. She looked me right in the eye as she did. No waffling. No lying. No keeping things from me. "When I left you at Delphine's, we went to rent this to transport her."

"Transport her where?" I asked. I wasn't sure what I should be feeling, but a small part was happy she tried to do *some*thing.

"Arizona." The Duke looked away, then, and stared at the wall over Delphine's head. "If we could have kept ahead of the FBVA, maybe we would've stayed together."

Tears burned behind my eyes, and I closed them to take a deep breath.

"But I suppose none of that matters now," she said, lips lifting a little. "You two sure this drug of yours is a cure?"

"Not completely sure," Delphine piped up. "But it's the best thing we've got."

"Good." With a nod, the Duke met my eyes again. "Because when we got back to the house, Mama was stronger than before, more volatile, and we couldn't figure out how to get her from the basement to the truck without the entire neighborhood calling the police."

"The protection circle is weaker now?" I asked.

She shook her head. "No, I reinforced that after I dropped you off at Delphine's. It was like...she was changing. Becoming less...out of control. More able to focus on what she wanted to do."

My stomach flipped over as I thought of Mama. Angry, scared, alone, and something...new. Different. I wondered if it hurt, if becoming a super vampire was like getting a tooth, or growing an inch overnight, or...worse.

"Open your backpack, Sophie," Delphine said quietly. "Show her the ledgers."

I jerked back to reality and did just that.

"Do you have a way to administer the antidote?" Delphine asked, glancing at the Duke. "Something intravenous?"

Silence settled over the truck as my chest tightened. Why didn't we think of that when we were in the lab? There had to be needles lying around somewhere.

"Yes." My eyes widened as the Duke replied. "I still have all that medical equipment to extract blood from donors. There are a few unused needles in the kit."

It felt like the drive home took forever. Maybe because we were antsy and tense and just waiting for a cop to pull us over. But there was no one on the road.

"You two go upstairs and get some rest." The Duke sounded real tired as we piled into the dark foyer of our house.

"No way, I want to see—" I began, but she cut me off.

"It's three a.m."

All right. But I needed to make sure it worked. That Mama would be okay.

"Yes, I have her, Phil...." Delphine's mom was on her phone, talking to Delphine's dad. "Absolutely not...and she'll be punished.... Well, you better figure it out, because this isn't okay behavior.... No, we have to nip it in the bud now...."

Next to me, Delphine rolled her eyes and leaned toward me. "Poor Papa will be forced to confiscate my bobblehead collection before she's appeased."

I snort-laughed.

"Go on, Sophie. Upstairs. You too, Delphine. Your mom said she'd stay to help, bless her. I'm not sure what she can help with, but she's a wonderful person," said the Duke, as she placed a hand on Delphine's arm. "And, Sophie?"

I looked at her, her eyes fierce with something like . . . pride shining through. "Yes?"

"Whatever happens. We'll face it together. As a family."

That's all I needed. With a nod, I turned, grabbed the banister, and started up the stairs.

"When this is over, my daughter won't be allowed to hang out with yours ever again," Delphine's mom said sharply. I smiled, and Delphine groaned, right behind me on the stairs.

"Delphine is three hundred years old, Susan." The Duke laughed. "If anyone led anyone astray, it was *your* daughter."

Chapter 29

That night I had nightmares. Of being chased, of being killed, of losing Delphine and the Duke and Mama, and even Delphine's mom.

But I couldn't say I didn't sleep well, because when my eyes finally fluttered open, it was four in the afternoon.

Crap! I sat up and threw off the covers, heart pounding as I looked around the room. There was no sign of Delphine, even though we'd both slept in my bed.

Or maybe we hadn't.... Had I dreamed that too? Shaking my head, I reached for my phone—it was charging on my nightstand—and typed out a message to the Duke.

> I'm awake.

I scrambled from bed—still wearing the black leggings and hoodie from the night before—and, grabbing a hairbrush, brushed my hair.

All right. I could do this. I could. I just had to leave my room, go downstairs, and . . . see what happened. Right?

But my heart raced, putting pressure on my chest until my breath came in fast, shallow pants. It was that same "couldn't breathe" feeling I had when we met Simon, and I sat back down on the bed.

I couldn't do it. I couldn't go down there if things had gone wrong. Not after everything I'd done, and been through. Not after—

A knock scared the heck out of me, and I jumped.

"Kiddo?" It was the Duke. With . . . bad news? Good news?

Oh God. A lump formed in my throat, but I croaked around it.

"Come in."

The door opened, and there she was. Pristine as ever, hair pulled back in a soft, single braid. She smiled. Really smiled. Like a full-on headlights kind of smile.

"What? What happened?" I asked. I didn't want to get excited, but if it was bad news she probably wouldn't be smiling like that.

"Got your text."

Well, obviously. "How's Mama?"

And her smile got even bigger. "Everything is fine. She's a bit weak, but Susan gave a pint of her blood before she left, and Mama's stronger now than when she woke."

"It worked?" I didn't know whether to laugh or cry or maybe scream with joy.

"You saved the day, kiddo."

Butterflies fluttered in my stomach as I smiled, and the Duke sat next to me on the bed.

"Come here," she said, wrapping her arms around me. Then she squeezed, and I *did* laugh. "It was rough trying to give her the antidote, but once I did, she drifted off to sleep nice and easy. Then it was just a waiting game to see what happened. But don't you ever, ever do anything like that again. Next time, you come to me. Don't feel like we can't talk, or we're going to have one heck of a time in high school."

I wasn't sure what she meant, but I was so happy it didn't matter. "I promise." I grinned into her shoulder and squeezed her back.

"Now, Delphine is in my office. We've been scanning those ledgers into my computer all morning while Mama was sleeping it off." She pulled away. "But I wanted to wait for you before we sent them anywhere. I've had my legal team reading them all morning, and they've given the green light."

"Wait...you left Delphine alone? With a *computer?*"

She arched an eyebrow. "Umm...yes?"

"Then we better get down there before it's all accidentally uploaded to social media."

The Duke chuckled, and I smiled. "What about Asger? If he's alive, won't he run?"

She shrugged. "Probably. But I also called Aaheru, who was as shocked as poor Delphine to find out he was still alive, and glamouring his appearance all these years. If Asger runs, Aaheru will send hunters after him. Don't worry about that. Just know the people in the FBVA facility should be out of there very soon. And that's all because of you."

I'm not sure what made my chest feel all warm and full, but hearing that definitely made me feel good. The choice to leave them behind had been hard, but it was for the best, because I *couldn't* help them last night. It wasn't the right time.

"Come on." The Duke stood and held out her hand. "Let's check on Delphine, then we'll see if Mama is ready for visitors."

"Where is she?" I asked, ignoring the tears in my eyes. "Mama?"

"She was freshening up when I left her, but she'll meet us in the living room."

"Then what are we waiting for?" I asked.

The Duke laughed. "Let's go."

"I'm insulted. Honestly." Delphine rolled her eyes as I sat in the Duke's office chair. "As if I could be clumsy enough to send any of this to the wrong people."

I laughed, my lips pulled into a smile so wide it hurt.

"It's two hundred fifty pages total." With a nod, and a smile of her own, Delphine pointed to the computer screen.

"Did you read any of it?" I asked, squinting at the computer.

"We did." The Duke stepped bchind the chair and placed cool hands on my shoulders. "The scheme was quite nefarious."

Uh . . . "nefarious" was probably bad.

"Turns out, Asger used his own blood to create the rogue formula, so he could manage the affected vampires." Delphine scowled and crossed her arms over her chest. "It was like he was thc one who turned them into vampires in the first place—which gave him control over them."

I remembered the way Delphine couldn't use her power when Asger held her wrist. "But he had to touch your skin to control *your* power."

"Yes. But whatever he did in the lab allowed him to control them with his mind."

"Wow." My eyebrows arched.

"The plan was to eventually turn *all* vampires rogue." The Duke sighed, and I glanced over my shoulder. Her lips were pressed together, so hard her jaw clenched.

"But it's all okay now," I said, my voice soft. She looked at me, and the ghost of a smile transformed her face.

"It is, Sophie-Bear." She bent to kiss the top of my head. "All right. You do the honors."

"Me?" My eyes widened.

"Of course you." Delphine grinned. "This was your plan, silly. You should be the one to hit send."

My heart fluttered in my chest as I turned back to the computer. The Duke had typed up an email, and there were lots of attachments, but my gaze shifted to the top. To the "to" and "cc" fields.

The Department of Justice.

The Department of Homeland Security.

The secretary of defense.

The . . . president of the United States.

And a ton of news stations were cc'd.

My hand shook as I placed it over the mouse, and I cleared my throat.

"Together," I murmured, glancing at Delphine before nodding at the mouse. "We do it together."

With a smile, Delphine's cool hand covered mine, and we both guided the cursor on the screen to the SEND button.

"On three," I said. "One."

"Two." Delphine's fingers tightened around mine. "Three."

And with a quick squeeze, Delphine and I sent the evidence of everything to the most powerful people in the country.

Delphine said she'd stay in the office while I went to see Mama—to keep an eye on any replies. She looked so funny, scowling at the screen as if expecting everyone to reply within minutes.

"It could take a while," I said, smiling as I walked to the office door.

"Yes, yes, I know." Delphine winked before turning back to the computer. "Go see your mama."

I didn't have to be told twice. Heart fluttering, I left the office.

"Mama!" I called, jogging down the hall.

"Slow down, silly goose," the Duke said, following me.

I laughed and threw a smile over my shoulder. Because Mama was okay. The prisoners would be released. And everything would be fine. I said it over and over in my head as I zipped into the living room, focused on the back of the chaise.

The big, old TV was on, and a black-and-white movie played. I recognized it but couldn't remember the name. I never paid much attention to Mama's shows, but maybe I would now. Just to be closer to her. To *feel* closer to her.

"Mama?" I called again, and a head lifted from the chaise. I came to a stop and froze. Her hair was . . . perfect. She must have showered and fixed it, and the thought made me giggle. Only Mama would've gone through what she did and then decide the most important thing was to make herself presentable.

"Baby!" she exclaimed, her voice a little hoarse. But it was her. I ran, rounding the chaise before throwing myself into her outstretched arms. "Oh, my Sophie. My love. My life."

Kisses rained on my hair, my forehead, my cheeks, and the tears I'd ignored in the bedroom flowed down my face.

"Mommy." I sobbed, melting into her cool-to-the-touch embrace.

"It's all right, baby. Everything's going to be all right," she soothed as the Duke joined us on the chaise.

And then there were two sets of arms around me, hugging, comforting, and it was like nothing bad had happened at all. As if it were just a family group hug for my birthday or the holidays, or just a "super well done" for test scores.

Because this was who we were, and nothing would ever come between us again.

That's when the doorbell rang, and Mama pulled back a little.

"Who might that be?" she asked, turning to the Duke.

"I imagine that's Laura, and the FBVA with their warrant."

Ugh. I'd almost forgotten about that.

"Well," Mama said brightly, even though her

voice was scratchy. "Let's go answer that door as a family, so I can give her a piece of my mind. And *thank* her for caring so much about our baby girl that she went to all that trouble. Even if I'm a little insulted."

"You *were* rogue, my love," said the Duke.

"But not anymore." Mama smiled. "And now no one will ever go rogue again."

Chapter 30

Mama welcomed Laura the second she opened the door, which was funny, because Laura was too surprised to speak. She really wasn't expecting to see Mama at all, and to watch her go almost as pale as my parents was something I'd remember for a really long time.

Victory. But the Duke still allowed them all to come in and check the house, all polite and respectful, with no hard feelings.

Mama told Laura where she'd been—my moms had obviously talked long before I'd woken up—and Laura left satisfied, though she knew things weren't one hundred percent okay between her and my parents. Mainly because Mama didn't offer up a single refreshment. No cookies. No sandwiches. Not even a glass of water. I mean, Mama was also too weak to go making cookies or sandwiches, but that didn't matter. It was a Bad Sign, and Laura knew it, because Mama always said offering food and drinks was just good manners.

And with Mama not being able to do much, I *finally* had the chance to cook for myself, and I think I did a pretty good job.

But school was rough. It's not like I was out for long, only two days all week, but when the news broke about what was happening in the FBVA facility, it was all anyone talked about on Friday. By lunchtime, the president of the United States had issued an order demanding the release of all family members imprisoned there, and he'd had doctors administer the antidote to the rogue vampires before addressing the nation.

All sale of synthetic blood was to stop, and any vampire with synthetic blood in the house should toss it and contact their local hospital for organic blood bags.

Humans were *so* upset and outraged by everything that by Saturday, the day of the blood drive, there was a line outside the blood bank that ran the entire length of the plaza. And camera crews. And reporters.

The Duke and I had driven through the parking lot just to get a look at it before making our way to Chuck's to meet Delphine.

"There's Delphine."

I saw her right as she said it—Delphine dressed as usual in a bouncy skirt and blouse, complete with an umbrella for shade—and unbuckled my seat belt before the Duke had put the Mercedes in park.

"Wait for me," she said, but I was already opening the door. Delphine hadn't been at school Friday, and I hoped she was okay.

I ran, full speed, and yelled her name.

But she was far too refined to wave. Instead, she smiled beneath the shadow of her umbrella and raised a hand. "There you are!"

I laughed and threw my arms around her.

"Oh my," she said, waiting a second before returning my hug.

"Are you okay?" I asked, whispering in her ear. "You weren't at school yesterday."

"I...I think I will be," she replied, pulling back to look at me. "When I got home, everything just hit me like a ton of bricks, you know? Seeing Asger... I don't know. It dredged up all these memories. And then what I said to you, how I acted in Asger's office."

My eyes locked with Delphine's, and I noticed the telltale signs of pre–bloody tears.

"That's already forgotten about. Seriously. Besides... maybe you were right," I said. "I...I think I want to write her back...Tara. And just, I don't know. Start a conversation."

I'd been thinking a lot about it since Laura had left our house and things settled down. My parents loved me, and reaching out to Tara wouldn't put my family life in danger. My family was my family, no matter what.

Delphine smiled a little. "I think that's a good idea. I decided to talk to a therapist about all this.

Honestly, I could've used one when I was first turned into a vampire."

"Well, thank goodness for the twenty-first century then." I chuckled.

Delphine shook her head. "Lord, when I think about how you sprayed Asger with the garlic."

"Right in his face," I said, and Delphine laughed. I placed an arm around her shoulder. "You should've seen the line at the blood bank. It was like the whole town showed up to donate."

"Unbelievable," Delphine said. "I'd love to see it. But first, let's get you an iced hot chocolate."

"We did all this." I didn't think that had really sunk in until that moment. We did this. That thought was so big I couldn't wrap my head around it as I followed Delphine into the familiar warmth of Chuck's. "Did you message Simon? Did you tell him?"

"I *did*." Delphine grinned. "I think his words were 'you two kick butt.' Anyway, he said his dad was relieved, and I watched the governor give an impassioned speech this morning on the television. As predicted, he told the world that he was shocked and appalled. And he plans on passing a ton of laws to ensure the blood supply never runs low, starting with reinstating the blood transaction payments. Oh! And outlawing the curfew!"

"That's *great* news!"

"Of course, the president ordered a full investigation." Delphine's eyes widened. "Oh! And Simon mentioned he'd like to meet up with us soon. He wants a step-by-step account of everything."

I smiled. "Sounds awesome."

The café was unusually quiet, probably because people were over at the blood bank. We didn't even have to wait in line.

"What can I get you?" asked the cashier with a smile.

"An iced hot chocolate, please," I said, as the bell over the door tinkled. I glanced over my shoulder. It was the Duke.

"And for you?" I turned in surprise as the cashier looked at Delphine. Delphine pursed her lips, then chuckled.

"I don't think you have anything for me back there, but thank you," she said.

The cashier smiled. "I can't tempt you with a

mug of gently warmed O-negative? The boss went down to the blood bank this morning and grabbed a few bags."

My eyebrows arched as Delphine's jaw dropped.

"Make that two O-negs, please," the Duke said, approaching. "On me."

"Great!" The cashier beamed as the Duke inserted her card into the payment terminal. "The owners are trying to get the right kind of refrigeration units for long-term storage, so it'll be a regular thing." She winked at Delphine. "We want to make sure *all* our patrons can enjoy Chuck's Chocolate House."

"Wonderful news," said the Duke, grinning as we moved down the counter to the serving area.

"I...wow." Delphine shook her head, her eyes a little bloodshot as she glanced at me. "Blood at Chuck's. I honestly never thought I'd see the day."

"It's a whole new world. *And* the president of the United States is working hand in hand with the Vampire Council," the Duke said with a chuckle. "*That's* a new one. He even gave Aaheru an official task force to hunt down Asger."

"Do you suppose they'll find him?" Delphine bit

her lower lip as the barista slid my iced hot chocolate across the counter.

Asger had run, just like we thought he would. When the military stormed the FBVA facility, he was gone.

"Oh, certainly," said the Duke, smiling as the barista returned with two warmed mugs of O-negative. "Thank you."

"A toast? To Sophie," Delphine said, raising her mug. "Our heroine, without whom none of this would be possible."

"To Sophie," the Duke echoed, and I felt my cheeks turn bright red.

"And to Delphine." Duh. I lifted my iced hot chocolate. "Because we couldn't have done this without both of us."

"Oh, take a compliment, Sophie Dawes," Delphine said with a snort before turning to the Duke.

"You both did an amazing job," the Duke agreed. "To the future."

To the future. Where we wouldn't have to worry about vampires going rogue, or getting thrown in a fake rehab facility ever again.

I smiled as we gently clinked our drinks together.

That was the kind of tomorrow I wanted, and not just for me. For my family, and for vampires everywhere.

Because vampires and humans were stronger together.

And I'd always make sure my family could walk in the light.

Acknowledgments

As I began writing *The Last Hope in Hopetown*, I had no idea it would become my debut novel. They say it takes a village ... but in my case, I had a city.

Thank you to my incredible literary agent, Amy Giuffrida. You saw something in Sophie and made it your mission to get *The Last Hope in Hopetown* into the hands of readers. I'm so grateful that we found each other and that I have a champion for my work. Here's to this book and many more to come. Likewise, thank you to my brilliant editor, Liz Kossnar, and the entire team at Little, Brown Books for Young Readers—especially the assistants working hard behind the scenes: Jéla Lewter and Aria Balraj. I don't know why you chose my work amid an ocean of other incredible stories, but you did. Thank you for believing in me. And to my cover artist, Bex

Glendining—thank you for bringing this world I created to life.

For this book, in particular, I have some very special people to thank: my army of middle-grade beta readers, ranging in age from seven to twelve. Logan Manzano, you are a ray of sunshine and one of the most intelligent, loving kids I've ever had the privilege of knowing. Don't let anyone, or anything, dim your light. You are strong. You are brave. You are worthy. To Amos, Sheldon, and Jonas—thank you so much for your input. And thanks to your incredible mom—author and personal friend, S. Kaeth—for allowing you to be part of this process.

To my freelance editor, colleague, friend, mentor, queen, surrogate sister/aunt/mom (depending on the day), fellow crone, the other half of our dastardly duo—*takes a breath*—the incredible powerhouse, Jeni Chappelle. I don't know where I'd be today without your love, encouragement, and guidance. Thank you for yelling at me to write *The Last Hope in Hopetown* and for being there every step of the way over the course of our years together. You are my beacon in the storm. You took this lonely, fractured immigrant and adopted me into your heart. For that, I'll be forever grateful. We are the definition of found family, even if there are multiple state lines between us.

To the Manzanos (more found family)—Ismael, Justine, Megan—because you're all amazing writers, editors, and literary agents! Justine and Ismael, you're incredible parents to an amazing kid; and Megan, you're the best aunt Logan could ask for. Thank you for teaming up with me all those years ago. You improved my writing. And Ismael...I can *still* hear your voice in my head when I self-edit.

To Revise & Resub (#RevPit) and the RevPit community—thank you for continuing to allow me to be part of this incredible force in publishing. And many thanks to the entire writing community on Twitter.

To those who were there from almost the beginning, my very first beta readers, Kelly Taylor and Natalie Tureaud. Thank you from the bottom of my heart. Your unwavering support meant—and still means—everything to me.

Very special thanks to Aoife Doyle, Beck Erixson,

Belinda Grant, Sierra Pung, and Ashley McAnelly for checking in on me. You all keep me going.

To the authors in my life who are in contact daily as we navigate the minefield of publishing—Paulette Kennedy, Jessica Lewis, Thuy Nguyen, and Esme Symes-Smith. Your love and support mean the world to me.

To my agent siblings—Jenny Perinovic, Taylor Kemper, Haley Hwang, Mary Lynne Gibbs, Rebecca Barto, Teagan Olivia Sturmer, Sarah Elynn, Sasa Hawk, Sarah T. Dubb, Jax McQueen, Catherine Harry, Jenn Roush, Jen Ruddock, K. M. Walton, and Chelsea G. Parker—thank you for your unwavering support. I'm honored to be part of the A-Team!

To all my writing groups and their members, particularly Writer in Motion (WIM). Thank you for being there for me when I needed you—Jenna, Megan, HM, Susan, Kathryn, Sher, Melissa, CQ, Kristen. And a special shout-out to K. J. Harrowick, who is also an incredible website designer.

To the other members of the Sisterhood of the Traveling Pantsers (you superstars)—Raquel Miotto and Ari Augustine—thank you for the love and encouragement.

To all the literary agents who have been so supportive of my work and career over the years—Tara Gilbert, Uwe Stender, Hannah Van Vels, Kaitlyn Johnson, James McGowan, and Eric Smith. Thank you for taking an interest in me and for helping in so many ways as I navigated my way toward this debut.

To Mam—you never stopped believing in me. Thank you for giving me the gift of reading from a young age, and thank you to whatever angel kept you safe when I thought I would lose you forever. I'm so incredibly grateful and happy you're here to share this moment with me.

To my sister, Sara. This book is dedicated to you because you're my Delphine—wise, a little dangerous (ha ha), and you always have my back. I miss you more than you know or could fathom. You are my strength and the half of my heart that aches with emptiness. I can't wait to meet Freddie in person!

To Dad—you taught me the meaning of hard work, and I never forgot that lesson. Thank you.

And finally, to the half of my heart filled with love and light—Devon. You're the best son a mother could want or need. The quest to fulfilling my dreams was a slog of long workdays and even longer nights as I snatched a few hours to write while you slept. I didn't even realize it before you were born, but everything I've worked toward is for you. And to Dan—you didn't quite appreciate all the writing when the dishes piled up, but you never wavered in your support when you saw how happy it made me. Thank you for being there. I love you both.

Maria Tureaud

hails from the Wild Atlantic Way on the west coast of Ireland. A developmental editor of fourteen years, Maria serves on the board for Revise & Resub (#RevPit on Twitter), an organization dedicated to uplifting the writing community. When she's not writing books or sprinkling magic into client manuscripts, you can find her drinking tea in New Jersey with her husband and son as she dreams of moving home to her beloved County Clare.